The Hood Samaritan

The Hood Samaritan

WHAT HAPPENS WHEN THE KINGDOM OF GOD INVADES THE HOOD

Roc Origen &
Derek Martyr

iUniverse, Inc.
Bloomington

The Hood Samaritan

WHAT HAPPENS WHEN THE KINGDOM OF GOD INVADES THE HOOD

iUniverse books may be ordered through booksellers or by contacting:

iUniverse
1663 Liberty Drive
Bloomington, IN 47403
www.iuniverse.com
1-800-Authors (1-800-288-4677)

ISBN: 978-1-4620-7261-3 (sc)
ISBN: 978-1-4620-7262-0 (ebk)

Printed in the United States of America

iUniverse rev. date: 02/08/2012

ACKNOWLEDGMENTS

To the very first Hood Samaritan—Jesus Christ. My Savior, my Lord, my Life–I love you. I really appreciated your patience with me. Each day I'm growing more confident in you; that you will complete that work you begun in my life. I could never ever repay you for laying down your life for me. I could only follow your example, laying my life down for your sake.

To my heart, my soul, the love of my life–Shonda Taylor. ALL that I ever wanted and need in this world, God has placed in you. Thanks for seeing all the things in me that no one else could. It took special eyes like yours. I also appreciate all your endless patience, support, and hard work. And I look forward to an exciting journey serving God besides you.

To the world's number one parents–Bertnella and Christopher Taylor. Without you there is no me. Your love is endless and I love you back. Your lives have instilled in me a lifetime of love, wisdom, and determination to be the best I possibly can at whatever I do.

To the most amazing mother-in-law I could ever know—Carolyn Powell. You have a heart of gold and I love you. Thanks for all your help editing the manuscript. God Bless You.

To Jamel Powell. Keep ya head up. Look up to the hills from where your help comes. And don't ever stop calling on the name of Jesus. With God, nothing is impossible.

Welcome home Cleon! Be patient and keep your eyes on the prize. Godly blessings always come to those who wait on Him.

Special Acknowledgments to Cousin Janet, Carla, Sher, Janelle (thanks for all your help), Miesha, Neil, Cadell, Mike, Karnisha, Michelle, Jackie, Terry-Ann, Kevin, Carolyn, Dwayne, Earl, Mark, June, Cozy, Fred, Phoenix, and Leelo and Pat. I could never forget ya'll.

To all the godly soldiers rising in the East. Dee, you already know what it is. I appreciate everything. Young, Twin, Rob, Darryl, Terry, Joe G.I., Antar, Emmanuel, Rippy, Chris, Isaac, Preacher White, Minister John Redding, Grace and Peace, Alex, Oscar, Zapata, Will, Jay, Frankie, Phil, Lee, Killiebrewski, Baker, Ricky, Jay, Blessed, Zion and Jay Diaz. Continue to fight the good fight—as one.

Dedicated to—All the Hood Samaritans around the world. God hasn't forgotten you. In fact, He's closer than you think.

PROLOGUE

"Thank you Lord," hollered Donteer Brown, loud enough for his words to ricochet off the steel walls and through the bars that confined him for the past three years. He hardly had any sleep the previous night because, in his mind, he'd already began implementing his plans for him and his family as he spent his last night in a prison bed. Clearly, he was a better man, with brilliant focus, and a brighter outlook on life.

Donteer was very handsome, of dark complexion. He was humble yet serious looking. At five foot ten, and only one hundred eighty—five pounds, he wore a very non-threatening persona, especially for in the pens.

"Yo, what's poppin D?" asked Roque in his deep baritone voice, quickly snapping Donteer's attention back to the harsh realities of penitentiary life. He stood in front of Donteer's cell with only his state—issued green pants and black boots on, revealing his cuts and stab wounds covered over by jailhouse tattoos. "You going out to the yard tonight?"

Rogue was in his late forties. At six foot four inches, two hundred seventy-five pounds solid, ball-headed, charcoal-black, with a long ugly slash from the outside corner of his right eye to just over his right ear. He resembled something that came straight out of the Congo. His body full of tats only made him look a little more humane. Even looking at him now, Donteer was reminded that at one time, Rogue was that dude who was always scheming. He was that crab in the barrel, that shark in the pool, that gorilla in the jungle, that jungle known to most outsiders as Sing Sing Correctional Facility.

"Man, you crazy or something?" Donteer asked him, incredulously, while still laying on his bed with his hands clasped behind his head. "The only yard I'm hitting is in them streets tomorrow with my family. I can't afford to jeopardize that. They need me right now, Rogue, more than anyone."

More than anyone, Rogue knew the daily hazards that came along with Sing Sing's yard—where the predators prey. At one time he had took part in its allurements, setting traps for the young and weak minded individuals, luring them in, and feeding on all of their resources. The yard was where it all went down. He had seen the new heads come through, their first time upstate, sucked into drugs, gambling, or just the wrong crowd, only to leave in a worse state than they had originally came in. He'd seen the older veterans, who were more familiar with the system, skate through their entire bid, only to get stabbed or killed their last week before they went home. He had also noticed that Donteer . . . was different.

"Yeah, I feel you. You don't need to get yourself caught up in nothing," he told Donteer, stretching out his right arm through the bar. "Do the right thing out there just like you did in here."

Donteer jumped up from the bed and met Rogue with his right hand, giving him a pound through the cell bar. "No doubt, Rogue, it was good to meet you big bro," he told him. "Wish it would've been under better circumstances but . . . it is what it is."

"God bless you and your family. You'll be all right. You got a good head on ya shoulder. Just stay focused out there. I let you slide out the back door this time, but if I see you in here again . . ."

Donteer held up his hand. "Wont happen . . . trust me. Next time you'll see me is when you hit the streets so you stay focused in here. Your day is coming soon too, big bro."

Rogue smiled, once again noticing the young brother's determination.

As Donteer looked Rogue in his eyes, he had to admit, he was gonna miss him. Rogue was a true gangsta turned Christian. He had grew tired of the grit and the grime and had decided to change his life right around the same time he had met Donteer, who was also desperately trying to build a relationship with Jesus Christ. Donteer respected Rogue a lot, and the courage it took for someone like him to actually claim Jesus as his Lord. Rogue's feelings were mutual. He liked how the young brother came through, stayed focused, placed God first in everything, went to school, planned for his future, and was truly ready when his time came.

"I got mad love for you, D. I appreciate everything."

"I love you too big bro."

With that, Rogue left. Saying goodbye was always hard among true friends, they both thought, as Donteer went back to his original position and Rogue went to his cell to prepare for the yard breakout.

Donteer pulled out his folder with everything he had accomplished since he was in prison. He pulled out his resume and his plan sheet, briefly going over his plans that would take affect the very next day, he thought. But as he laid there on his bed, he couldn't help backtracking through his entire life for the last time, for very next day his life his future would begin.

CHAPTER 2

Before going to prison, Donteer really wasn't a bad guy. Of all his friends, he was more of a leader. He was brought up in a two-family home, completed High School and earned an Associates degree in Liberal Arts before the age of twenty-one, and also held a few blue collar jobs. Unlike many young men growing up in the hood, he actually saw himself starting a family and moving on to a better life. So much so that immediately after graduating from college he married his High School sweetheart, April, and they had two beautiful kids; Jamal and Keesha.

From High School, Donteer and April just seemed to blend perfectly. She was a few months younger than him with a little more fervor for living. Coming from a single parent home, with no positive male figures in her life, she was easily drawn towards Donteer. She loved his sense of purpose and responsibility during school, the fact that he didn't hang out much with the fellas, that he was respectful to his teachers, and also to the young ladies who flirted with him. Being very handsome, street-smart, and funny, there was always some cutie with their eyes on him, who Donteer, quite politely, would always brush off. But April wasn't at all threatened by their advances, neither was she tottered. The foundation they shared was solid. She was confident in his feelings for her. They were consistent, and they grew. And she knew that at the end of the day he was coming to pick her up from class to take her home. Then he himself was going home to study his schoolwork, because he had direction. The two of them were a match made in heaven; he had vision, and her, motivation.

It was after graduating High School together that April and Donteer had their, Jamal. Even though they spoke about having kids, they didn't exactly plan his birth. But it was okay. Everything was still going according to plans. If anything, this hastened their plans for their future. It brought that much needed cohesion between the two, bringing out a sense of familial responsibility and the need for them to work together as a unit.

After Jamal's birth April left her parents and moved into Donteer's parents' home to share the responsibility and save money. Initially, they both worked but with a baby in the picture, April had to stay home and play mommy. Sometimes Donteer's parents, Mildred and Leonard, would help out, but Donteer, not wanting to appear irresponsible, didn't encourage this. He'd rather work two jobs if he had to, to cover the bills while April took care of young Jamal.

Everything was still going according to plans when a year later baby Keesha appeared. They were both looking at her like, 'Where'd you come from?' This was definitely not in their plans—not now—especially since their relationship was already somewhat strained. Being that Donteer was working at least fifteen hours a day, little time was left for him to reaffirm their future, restrengthen their bond, and to reassure his love for her, especially after giving birth to their first-born. And now there's Keesha.

Amazingly, they worked through it. This was a test of their love, as all relationships do have. In fact, most relationships collapse at this point. But Keesha's birth, if anything, brought more balance to their family. Donteer loved them, and cherished his role as a father and husband. He never gave up, but tried even harder. He got his parents even more involved in their grand-children's lives. And he even cut back to one job to make time for his kids and to support his wife, but this decision set him back financially, making him unable to move his family out of his parents' home.

Somewhere during this time, Donteer began spending time with his homeboy Tariq from up the block. They'd actually known each other since childhood but grew apart because of a lack of similar interests. But since he felt overburdened with his responsibilities, Donteer got away from time to time. And he hung out mostly with his boy Tariq.

❋ ❋ ❋

Tariq Parker was a hustler. He did it all. From selling drugs, to pulling stickups, to hitting the gambling spots, he spent all of his waking hours trying to get money. With both of his parents being drug addicts, and eventually dying in a car accident, Tariq was left in the care of his grandmother from a very young age. And, Lord knows, she couldn't control him. She had a hard enough time trying to deal with the loss of *her* husband. However, she spent most of her time praying for her grandson, hoping that one day he'll come around.

But Tariq just loved the streets. He felt as though he was born in 'em and raised by 'em. Like Donteer, he was also a leader; very confident and assertive, but very manipulative as well. He loved power, and reveled in being in control. And he soon became very good at it. He just never managed to make it past the street corner level with his multiple street trades. Over time, however, Tariq did become influential in his corner of the hood, but simply couldn't seem to become the big time hustler that his dreams portrayed. So for the time being, he was stuck with being small time, hustling and manipulating the little homies on the corner. His main homeboys were Brooklyn and Redd. And then there was Donteer.

❋ ❋ ❋

Brooklyn and Redd, aka Night and Day for their opposites in skin color, aka pm and am because they were always one behind the other everywhere they went, were ex-cons, also stuck in the cycle of the prison system. Not only could they not stay out of prison, but they couldn't stay off the corner, which, for them was the gateway back to the pens. They stood there day and night, and their absence for more than two weeks meant that they were behind bars.

❋ ❋ ❋

Hanging with Donteer brought a sense of balance to Tariq's life; balance that he needed to stay out of prison. In the hood, young men like Donteer are rare. As unfortunate as it was, most of his peers envied him and guys like him. They scorned his strength against opposition, his direction amidst confusion, and his astounding ability to ascend above adversity. This was Brooklyn's beef with Donteer. But Tariq, being a hustler, saw Donteer as an asset and decided to keep him close. He liked Donteer's style. Even if it was just to stop by for a few minutes on his way to the corner, Tariq made it his duty to holla at his boy D. However, because they didn't have much in common, their conversation usually ended with Tariq trying to get Donteer involved in the street life. And usually this was where they parted ways, because Donteer had a vision for his life which was far beyond the streets of Bedstuy.

And so it was, unlike most other hoods, the streets of Bedstuy, Brooklyn, were a microcosm of tenement buildings and private houses, a milieu of middle and lower class citizens, and a mixture of structured valued systems and those who are simply caught up in the system. And this was the climate that contributed to Donteer's life. Though he himself wasn't a bad person, he was a magnet for those around him who were stuck in bad situations. And though it seemed to make him a better person, as gold tried in the furnace, Donteer stayed in the fire. It was as though the more positive energy he put forth, the more negative came back. And the more he tried to move his family forward, the more the dark forces opposed him, sometimes even from within himself.

CHAPTER 3

It was the day Donteer would never forget when him and his wife, April, were coming from the corner store, and Tariq was hanging out with the homies. Tariq stopped Donteer, urgently needing to holler at him. April kept walking slowly as Tariq and Donteer walked a few steps behind. Tariq was asking Donteer to borrow five thousand dollars to cop some crack so that he can flip it. He presented his request to Donteer as an investment in order to first get Donteer's attention. He told Donteer that his investment would kick back ten thousand in two weeks. He told him he had a new spot that would bring in money 24/7, but he just didn't have any drugs. He even told Donteer that he didn't have to do anything, that Brooklyn and Redd would be doing all the work. To Donteer, this was an offer hard to refuse.

Donteer stopped from time to time, listening intently to the details of Tariq's offer. He was thinking that he can use some extra cash to help move April and the kids out of his parents' home. As they walked and talked, they stopped a couple more times.

The gap between Donteer and his wife then widened but she kept stopping and looking back, waiting for him to catch up. At one point, about halfway up the block, April stopped and was looking back when a man was walking towards her from the opposite direction. He approached her and tried to kick it. "Yo, what's up ma?" he said as he approached.

April had always turned a lot of heads, even more so now than in her teenage years. After two children, who were now pre-teens, she bloomed into an amazingly beautiful woman. With long wavy brown color hair and auburn streaks, her caramel complexion just scintillated and she filled out, doing justice to the clothes she wore. And at thirty years old, with two kids, she enjoyed the extra attention. She thought it was harmless.

After the man spoke to her, April turned and noticed the diamonds sparkling in his mouth as he smiled. *No he didn't*, she thought to herself, not even responding, her head turning back towards Donteer and Tariq. She was hoping that he'd get the point and continue about his business. "What's your name, sweetheart?" he continued, feeling prompted to press the issue.

Again no response. Only, this time she looked at him a little longer, thinking to herself, Dude you can't be serious.

❋ ❋ ❋

As Donteer and Tariq finished their conversation, Tariq turned and headed back to the store. "Holla at me, D!" he reminded Donteer.

"I'll think about it," Donteer responded as he sped up.

While looking up the mildly crowded block in search of his wife, he saw April standing there with who seemed like a stranger trying to talk to her. He sped up.

* * *

By this time April still hadn't said one word. She hadn't gestured that she was interested. She didn't even smile, as some women in her position would do as to not appear rude. She simply stood there impatiently waiting for her husband.

"Sweetheart," he continued. "I'd love to take you out some time, but I can't if I don't know your name."

The man obviously wasn't going to give up without a fight. He saw what appeared to be an easy catch standing right before him. I mean, why else would she be standing there right before him looking fine as ever. If she wasn't interested she would have simply walked away or at least told him she wasn't.

"My name is irrelevant," April finally responded when she looked up the block and saw Donteer approaching quickly. She figured she had to say something before the situation spun out of control.

"To me it is," he countered immediately. "Why would you say such a thing baby?" he pursued, now attempting to grab her hand, but April pulled it away.

"I'm not your baby," she snapped, resisting him all together. "That's my husband right there."

When the man turned around, all he saw from his peripheral was Donteer's right fist across his jaw.

"No Don, stop!" April yelled, but didn't dare intervene.

Donteer was merciless as he whipped this poor fella into a pulp. And, as if something had gotten into him, he picked up a neighbor's garbage can, repeatedly smashing it over the man's already unconscious body.

It wasn't long before the cops came and were hauling Donteer off to the precinct. Needless to say, the man pressed charges and came to court, testifying that Donteer assaulted him. Fortunately for Donteer, his wife and neighbors also came and testified on his behalf; that he was in fact defending his wife. And the fact that he had a job and a college degree also worked in his favor. Although the judge found Donteer guilty of attempted murder, claiming that he could've killed the poor man, he understood that Donteer was a family man simply trying to protect his wife. Donteer was sentenced to three years and it was then that he was cast away in Sing Sing Correctional Facility where he would serve the duration of his time.

* * *

While in prison, Donteer thought about everything; about his life, his family, his freedom, and how he lost it all because of his seemingly submerged temper. He knew he wasn't a bad person, but this was a dangerous problem; a problem that he needed to get in check quick, or next time he probably wouldn't be so lucky. Life is funny, he thought, just a few months ago I was a family man, working and enjoying the company of my wife and kids, and now I'm a prisoner.

Choices . . . was his conclusion. Unlike most in prison who blamed *the system* for their downfall, Donteer knew full and well why he went through those doors. He wasn't like Tariq, who had no parental guidance growing up and was left to resort to the streetlife. Neither was he like Brooklyn and Redd, who were stuck in the system mentally. Donteer understood fully that it was his personal choice that landed him where he was. He could have dealt with his situation in a totally different way but he chose to lose his temper and handle his business. Up until that moment he considered himself to be a good person, above average, but here it was he was now numbered with the transgressors. And just that quick he was locked on the inside, hardly even able to look out; except maybe only to watch his back. He was now a prisoner . . . just another number discarded in the prison system.

To make matters worse, April was now left at home alone to fend for herself and the children. Luckily Donteer had some money saved, and his parents also lent their help whenever it was needed. But she missed him dearly. There was nothing or no one that could've replaced his presence in her life. She was so use to him always being around that now that he was gone she sank into a state of depression and lost all her enthusiasm.

Then, during one of her check-ups with her oncologist, she was told that there were traces of cancer in her breasts. This was a heavy blow, too much for her to handle all by herself. So, indirectly, and out of frustration, she blamed Donteer for not being there.

It all broke his heart. Not that she blamed him, but he felt that she was right. He was culpable for not being there. As her husband, Donteer knew deep down within that it was his responsibility to be there for his wife and children. He also knew that a man was not suppose to allow anyone, or anything, to prevent him from assuming this responsibility. And he knew that had it not been for that choice he made that day, he would've been there with them, working through their problems together as a family, the way it should be. Nonetheless she stuck by his side the entire time, as he tried to maintain a relationship with his entire family from behind bars.

For the remainder of his time in prison, Donteer was committed to changing his life. He shared his plans with April and his parents. His mom had already begun encouraging April to go to church, and to place her faith in Jesus, telling her that Jesus can heal her. She also encouraged Donteer to do the same. And eventually he started praying and reading his Bible.

Before long, Donteer accepted Jesus Christ as his Lord and Savior. He was broken, and began his relationship with the Lord humbly. He was skeptical of churches because he saw his mom and her friends dedicate their lives to the institution and their circumstances never changed. However, he had to admit that their lives did change for the better. Well, this time he was desperate; for his wife to be healed, and for his own life to change. And he gave his whole heart to Jesus.

The time just seemed to fly by. Between going to school, working out, and planning, Donteer seemed not to have time enough for himself. He didn't hang out that much, except for with his brother Rogue from time to time. He even went on to earn a Bachelor's degree in Business. Before he knew it, it was his time, time to come home and be with his family again. Oh, how he missed them; being a husband to his wife, a father to his kids, and a better son to his parents. This time when he came home he was truly focused, determined not to allow anything to come between him and his family again; and to provide an even better future than he had originally planned for them.

CHAPTER 4

Coming home was euphoric for Donteer. He smothered his kids and the rest of the family just about every chance he got, but was determined not to waste any more time. Unlike many men and women who come home from prison, who would also leave God behind, Donteer tried his best to bring his new relationship with Jesus from within his heart to those around him. He shared it with his kids, his parents, and most of all, his wife—especially his wife. She needed his love and support the most, Donteer thought. He even tried going to church a couple of times with his family but felt somewhat outcasted because he was an ex-con.

However, one thing was for sure, Donteer wasn't going to hang out with Tariq anymore. For the couple of months since he was home, he'd been purposely busy, trying to avoid him. He even had his mom lie and tell Tariq he was busy when he came by looking for him. Secretly he blamed Tariq for distracting him the day when the incident took place with his wife April. And though had it not been for his prison sentence Donteer knew he would not have been the new person that he was, he also knew he now had to guard himself from anyone or anything that could potentially come between him and God, and him and his family. He couldn't allow Tariq nor his goons to make him lose focus. But of course they didn't appreciate this.

Usually when someone just came back home from prison, it was customary for them to hit the hood hard and make their presence felt again. They would hit all the old and new hot spots, reuniting with all the homies, telling their prison war stories to show that they'd survived the ultimate rites of passage—the steel cage behind the wall. And their homies would tell them how the hood ain't been the same without them, and how they couldn't wait for them to come home. And they'd welcome them back into the streets with a lot of liquor, drugs, parties, and whatever else it took to draw them right back into the street life. And the cycle goes on.

Donteer wasn't interested in none of the above. Neither was he interested in wasting any time with any so-called homies. The only thing on his mind was finding a job and taking care of his family. But when Donteer came home and was ducking Tariq, Tariq felt slighted. And he shared his feelings with Brooklyn and Redd, how his suppose to be homeboy D came home and didn't even come to check him. "Matter of fact," he told them. "I think that dude ducking me. I don't know what's up with that." However, Tariq knew it was only a matter of time before they bumped heads. Donteer's first running with them was not with Tariq, but it was with Brooklyn and Redd.

* * *

It was a Thursday afternoon, while going to Pedro's to buy some groceries for April that Brooklyn just couldn't help himself. "Watch where you're going!" he said aggressively, as Donteer barely brushed him coming out of the store.

Brooklyn just couldn't stand Donteer. Just the sight of Donteer repulsed him. If Tariq or Redd asked him why he didn't like him, the most he could say was, 'I just don't like him.' But deep within there were a few hidden reasons for Brooklyn's hatred.

First off, Donteer made him feel less than a man, less than a responsible man, that is. Second, before Donteer went to prison, Tariq began spending more time on Donteer's parents' porch with Donteer. Sometimes they would even play basketball together in the park early in the mornings on the weekends. It was almost as though Tariq was becoming more and more disinterested with running with Brooklyn and Redd. So Brooklyn was jealous of Donteer. And third, Donteer's entire image, especially after Brooklyn saw him for the first time since he came home from prison, went against everything Brooklyn stood for. The tough-guy persona—Donteer was not intimidated. Neither did Brooklyn's jail-house build and body laden with mostly jail-house tattoos seem to impress Donteer. Donteer was slim and had no tats. Even Brooklyn's most aggressive role plastered on his gangsta grill didn't phase him.

Donteer simply side-stepped him, "Pardon me!" he stated and continued down the block.

As he walked away, the more laid-back Redd tried to calm Brooklyn down. "Yo be easy," he told him. "That's Tariq's man," he continued mockingly while smiling. Physically, Redd was a light-skinned version of Brooklyn.

Though blatantly opposite in personality, it seemed as though the more he hung around Brooklyn, the more he started to be like him. From time to time, with a little weed and Hennessey in his system he would act extra. Like Brooklyn, he too had the jail-house build and his red skin complexion filled with jail-house tattoos. But he wore a fitted hat over his durag, while Brooklyn was comfortable with just a durag.

"That use to be Tariq's man," Brooklyn responded quickly. "He's a lame now."

"Hard to tell, the way he bumping you and all that," Redd exaggerated. "What's up with Ta anyway? My uncle was telling me about this new spot out of town, in Pennsylvania, where we can get some real money. All we gotta do is get the drugs down there."

Brooklyn didn't respond. He just continued to stare at Donteer as he walked down the block.

Though Donteer knew that Brooklyn and Redd were thugs, he wasn't at all threatened by Brooklyn's reproach. To him, they were lost. They were ex-cons like himself, but, as sad as it was, they were unable to function in society. And they resorted to hanging on the corner as followers with no leader.

Him, on the other hand, knew where he came from and where he was going. He moved with a sense of purpose—a renewed one. And he just couldn't afford to get caught up now.

As he walked down the block, he waved at Tariq's grandmother, Mrs. Abigail Parker, as she inquired, "How goes the job search, Donteer?"

Mrs. Parker loved Donteer's positive attitude, both before and even more so after he came home from prison. She saw him grow up, and knew that he was going to be a responsible young man, respectful to his elders and taking care of his family. She just wished that some of those qualities could have rubbed off on her grandson Tariq.

"I'm still looking, Mrs. Parker," he cordially responded.

"Keep the faith," she encouraged him, as he walked a couple more houses to his parents' home.

Stepping into his home was one of those luxuries that reminded Donteer of the simple privileges of being a free man. It also reminded him of the urgency to get a job so that he can buy his own home for his wife and kids. Before he went to prison he had saved a good amount of money towards this goal, but with his recent hiatus, and April's medical bills, he had to put that home on hold until he became a little more financially stable. Thankfully, his parents were understanding.

Thus purchasing his own home, and his children's college education were the very next things on Donteer's agenda. His kids were indeed getting older, and they needed their own space. Not to mention, a more positive and productive kind of neighborhood also. Some of the kids in his hood were too grown, without respect for their elders or peers; by-products of the streets of Bedstuy; hopeless, and almost destined for failure like Tariq and his boys.

❋ ❋ ❋

CHAPTER 5

In the hallway of his parents' brownstone, Donteer summoned his boy, Jamal, "Peanut, come give me a hand!"

Donteer called him Peanut because of his little bean head. It always amazed him how such a small head can absorb so much information. But he loved his son. He was a good replica of Donteer, very respectable, obedient, and dependable. Amazing how fast his lil man was growing up.

"Hey dad," Jamal greeted anxiously.

"What's up?" Donteer gave him the groceries that April sent him for.

"Take this in the kitchen to your mother. It smells like she's started dinner."

Sensing his presence, April hollered from the kitchen simultaneously, "Don, did you get my food?"

"On its way, hon!" he hollered back, while walking into the living room where his daughter Keesha was. She was sitting on the couch with her hair half-braided, watching music videos. Donteer turned the volume down before he took a seat across from her. "What do you need, a hearing aid?" he asked in good humor.

"Huh?" she responded playfully. "No dad! Grandma and mom said it wasn't too loud."

"That's because they're way in the kitchen" he told her, "and don't want you eavesdropping on their conversation. I, on the other hand, can't hear myself think."

Keesha was very shy. She was over-weight, and had low self-esteem. But her dad always seemed to know how to fan that flame of confidence within her heart. Around him, she just knew she was beautiful and intelligent.

"Maybe you're not thinking," she wittily responded.

Donteer loved when she teased him. That was his babygirl. He knew that she was shy and had low self-esteem, but that was common among most girls her age, he figured. He just tried his best to provide a healthy environment for her to feel loved in order to develop her personality and self-confidence.

"Oh, you got jokes?" he said smiling. "That's good," he shot back, "they'll go good with your homeless look." He looked and pointed to her half-done hair while getting up.

"Kim was braiding it but she had to run home," she said, self-consciously holding the unbraided portion of her hair.

"I thought it was a new style," he punned, giggling as though he got the last laugh.

Keesha sucked her teeth as Jamal came back into the living room. He gave his father a high five and took a seat on the couch, as Donteer, still smiling, walked out of the room. But before he left, being that he was in such a good mood, Keesha pushed her luck.

"Oh yeah dad, can Mark come over tomorrow night?" she asked him, as he was almost out of the room. But Donteer wasn't that drunk with excitement. Wasn't no young rascal gonna move his way in around his babygirl—not if he can help it—and especially not Mark. Jamal had told him that he had no respect. And Donteer knew he was only after one thing. Without even looking back, his answer was emphatic.

"No!"

❋ ❋ ❋

Donteer then entered the kitchen where his wife and mom were preparing dinner. He walked up behind April, hugged her, and kissed her on the cheek. Then he kissed his mother, who was still setting the table.

The dinner table was adjacent to the kitchen. Donteer stood back absorbing the scene and sweet aroma of roasted cornish hens, deep fried chicken wings and legs, candied yams, collard greens, lasagna, and macaroni and cheese. Not to mention the pumpkin and sweet potato pies, still smoking, fresh out the oven.

"Dinner will be ready," said Mildred, "so you might as well go wash your hands and get your father."

Looking at all the prepared food, and rubbing his hands together, Donteer wasted no time. He scurried up the stairs to his parents' room.

❋ ❋ ❋

Donteer's father, Leonard, was very intelligent and strong, but also a very prideful man. He spent a lot of time alone. Since everyone in the house was so Christian, he felt as though he couldn't relate. So most times he would simply create his own world. He was reading a newspaper when Donteer entered the room.

"Hey dad," he said, peeking his head into the room then walking in. "Dinner's about ready."

Leonard smiled when he saw his son, got up and folded the newspaper. "Your children chased me up here. They wanted to listen to that saggy pants music."

"We gotta let them be children dad, because Lord knows, they're gonna be adults longer than they get to be kids."

"Ain't that the truth. Employed yet?" Leonard asked him.

"Not yet!" said Donteer, his tone suddenly changing to a somber one.

Coming home from prison and trying to gain employment had been a very discouraging experience for Donteer. Although he had prior job experience, his prison record seemed to overshadow it. It wasn't like he didn't try. He knew that now he was home, he was on a schedule to get a job and move his family out of his parents' home. But every place he went to for the past two months since he'd been home denied him employment for one reason or another. His father sensed his discouragement. "You know you could always come down and work at the factory with me," he invited him. "I can put a word in for you. I told you that."

"I went to school for business dad. I'd like to work in that field."

"I hear you son. I'm just saying, sometimes you gotta crawl before you can walk. Factory work is respectable work. I've been able to support your mother doing it for forty years."

"Yes you have dad. I didn't say there was anything wrong with it. I just need a good salary to take care of April's medical treatment bills, and to put the kids through school."

Leonard looked sympathetic, as he headed for the door. "You always make a good argument son, so I'll just say one more thing. Jesus was a carpenter way before anyone identified Him as Savior." With that said, they both left the room and walked down the hall in tandem.

"You can't use that argument dad," Donteer said, trailing his father. "You don't even go to church."

Leonard was tickled. "I got you with that," he said laughing. "Trying to disqualify me, that's the sign of a man on the losing end of a debate."

❋ ❋ ❋

"Father, thank you for your many blessings," Donteer began his prayer as everyone sat around the dining room table holding hands. "You have always held us down. We ask that You bless this food in the name of Your precious son Jesus. Bless it Lord! Amen."

"Amen," said everyone in concert, especially Mildred, who placed emphasis on her's. She was so proud of her son.

"I felt like I was seated in heaven," Leonard said, mocking Donteer good-humoredly as the kids snickered.

Donteer didn't mind the pun, but Mildred didn't appreciate it. She sensed her husband's sarcasm a mile away but held her peace. Besides they were all happy to have Donteer back home where he belonged. Ever since he'd been back home, the family had been celebrating thanksgiving-style for dinner, with all different assortments of meals.

"Don, try the lasagna," April said to Donteer, sitting right beside him. "I made it just for you."

"For me honey," Donteer replied, smiling back at his wife. He reached over and dug into the tray of lasagna. He then went further into it as if he was on a furlough. "Dad, you were right," he mumbled as he ate. "I think we are in heaven right now."

April blushed, as everyone including Leonard smiled.

CHAPTER 6

The next day was Friday. Donteer gave it another shot, spending the entire day looking for a job. As the day turned into night, the corner store was poppin as usual. The young women and guys were huddled up chitchatting. Brooklyn and Redd were smoking weed and talking covertly, as they observed small dice game taking place off to the side of the bodega. And, shaking the dice, with his chest out and all eyes on him, looking confident, almost intimidating, was Tariq.

"This is my last roll," he stated, shaking the dice in one hand held high in the air and a weed cigar held low in the other, which also held his black velour sweatpants from falling off his buttocks. Tariq was dark-skinned and very handsome, with a stocky build, and his hair was corn-rowed behind his back. He had his serious game-face on as he towered over his opponents. "I'm not gonna be out here all night chasing small money," he said. He rolled the dice. It was a four, five, six—celo. "Take that," he boasted. "All ya'll fools, cough it up!"

He collected money from everyone one by one as they reluctantly gave it up. He stopped playing, and went and stood with Brooklyn and Redd. He spoke to them briefly, then spun off into the bodega, as Brooklyn and Redd resumed their conversation.

Brooklyn and Redd were like Pinky and The Brain; always scheming and looking for a vic to rob. They were known stick-up kids. Tariq didn't like the fact that they brought heat to him, making the block hot, but oftentimes he condoned them because he profited from their exploits. On the other hand, they were good for business because they held him down like he was the president.

Immediately after Tariq stepped into the store, an old station wagon pulled up. It double-parked and a man of small stature got out. He looked very unassuming with a dress shirt, slacks, and sneakers on. It was obvious to everyone that he wasn't from around there.

As he headed towards the bodega looking back towards his car, Brooklyn nudged Redd. They looked at the station wagon and their eyes simultaneously landed on the packages in the back seat. Brooklyn just couldn't resist.

"Do you know him?" he asked Redd, as the man entered the store.

"Naw, I never seen him before," Redd answered.

"Me either, go see if he left the keys in the car!"

Brooklyn turned around, looked into the bodega, and turned back around as Redd walked over to the station wagon and peeped inside. He then looked back at Brooklyn and shook his head, indicating no.

The man came back out the store with nothing in his hands. He walked towards Redd, who was at the wagon, while Brooklyn closed in from behind.

"Excuse me cuz . . ." Brooklyn said as he approached from the rear.

The man stopped and turned around facing Brooklyn.

"You wouldn't happen to have a dollar to spare, would you?" Brooklyn asked.

"Sure," the man responded immediately.

He dug into his pocket and took out a wad of cash. Brooklyn and Redd's eyes grew wide as the man peeled off a five-dollar bill.

"Here take five!" he said generously. He passed it to Brooklyn, who took it with his left hand and snatched all the cash from the man's hand with his right hand.

"I'll take it all," Brooklyn demanded, looking the man in his eyes. "That feels much better in my hand," he continued still staring the man down. At the same time, Redd yoked him from behind as Brooklyn then punched him in the face and stomach. "Hold him while I get his keys!" Brooklyn rummaged through his pocket as the men on the corner all looked on at the robbery. Tariq then exited the store and watched as well, in shock. "Got em!" said Brooklyn. Redd let the unconscious man go. After which, he fell to the ground, his head crashing against the curb. Immediately it started bleeding, pooling up the street.

Quickly everyone scattered. The young men that were playing dice ran one way. Tariq walked away quickly, holding up his sagging pants and heading in the other direction. And Brooklyn and Redd jumped into the station wagon and drove off.

The man laid there helpless between the two cars when Pastor Daniel Kelly, pastor of Faith Community Church, Donteer's family church, peeked out of the bodega. He then waved his wife, Karen, out of the store. From outside the store, they both looked nervously at the stranger laying on the ground.

"Oh my God, Daniel, What happened?" she inquired nervously.

"It's none of our business," the pastor responded quickly. "Come on!" He led her, pulling her by the hand as they both hurried down the street to where their car was parked.

Next, two young women in their twenties, Lisa and Tiffany, saw him. However, they also turned away and walked back down the block.

A car then pulled up next to the victim. In it was Levi James, treasurer of Faith Community, who exited his car. He almost stepped on the man, who rolled over, groaned, and looked Levi in his face. "Ah . . . help me!" he mumbled, as more blood leaked from the side of his mouth. Levi hesitated for a moment, looked around, climbed back into his car, and sped off to another store.

❋ ❋ ❋

Down the block, Donteer had just parked the car. He had a long day; another busy day trying to find a job. As he exited his car, Lisa and Tiffany were hurrying by.

"Hey Lisa . . . Tiffany . . ." he greeted them, noticing how fast they were moving. "What's the hurry?"

Seeming almost excited to tell somebody, Lisa responded first. "Brooklyn and them just robbed somebody in front of the store. We went to go see. He looks like he's dying in the street."

Donteer looked down the deserted block to the corner, which was unusually empty.

"Yup," Tiffany then followed, "and Pastor Kelly walked right on by; didn't even offer a prayer. You better get off the street, Donteer. You know the cops around here will put that case on anybody they see."

Lisa and Tiffany hurried on, as Donteer quickly walked up the deserted block toward the store. He saw the man laid out in the street. He then ran over to him, stooped down, and cradled his head. "Are you all right?" Donteer asked, with concern in his eyes. "What happened?"

"I . . . can't . . . ahh." The man struggled, trying to respond as he slipped in and out of consciousness.

Donteer noticed and yelled for help. "Somebody help me!" he yelled out loud. "Call an ambulance."

CHAPTER 7

In the living room of Donteer's parent's home, Keesha was sitting on the couch with Mark. At fifteen years old, he was quiet, but shrewd and very sneaky. He spotted his victim, one of low self-esteem, and moved in, this time only for a kiss.

"My mother is in the other room," Keesha squirmed, resisting him.

"So," Mark responded nonchalantly.

He moved in to kiss her again. This time she didn't move away. They stopped only when the front door flew opened, and Donteer yelled.

"Somebody help me!" Donteer struggled through the door with the man over his shoulder, hoisting him up. The man attempted to walk but one foot dragged on the floor as they passed the home's threshold.

Immediately, April, Mildred, and Keesha came frantically to meet Donteer. They saw the stranger's chest and head covered in blood. They also saw blood on Donteer's shirt and hands.

"Daddy, what happened?" Keesha blurted, followed by his wife.

"Don, what happened?" she asked.

"I'm okay," he reassured them. "It's him. Just help me get him into the living room."

April helped her husband navigate the man into the living room. Donteer then made a motion like he wanted to put the man down on the couch, when Mildred panicked. "Not the couch!" she stated.

"Okay," responded Donteer, understanding her hysteria. "Lay him down on the floor slowly. Keesha get a pillow and a warm towel."

Hearing the commotion, Leonard and Jamal then came into the room looking surprised. "Donteer, what did you do?" questioned Leonard.

"Nothing dad, he got robbed on the corner. I just helped him."

"By bringing him here?" Leonard responded. He just couldn't believe his son's absurdity.

Keesha came back with a pillow and towel. Donteer took the towel and placed it under the man's head, wrapping the towel completely around it. Then Mildred, sensing her husband's discomfort, came with a cell phone and dialed a number. "I'm calling an ambulance," she said as she dialed.

"Son," Leonard continued. "Don't you think this was a mistake? If he's unable to tell the police what happened, who will—you? They're not gonna believe you. You're an ex-con."

Donteer thought for a second, filled with mixed emotions. He was confused and simply thought he was doing the right thing. After all, he did save someone's life. But what his father said seemed to make sense. He then felt even more embarrassed that his father would even speak to him that way in front of his kids. Then, to make matters worse, he looked over to his right and saw Mark standing next to his babygirl and a new emotion erupted within him.

"Go home!" Donteer snapped without skipping a beat, angry at just the sight of this kid next to his daughter.

Mark contended. "But your wife said . . ."

"I said go home!" Donteer spat once again. He was now agitated that he would even have the nerve to open his mouth to a grown man. "Don't talk back to me in my house."

Mark attempted to pierce Donteer with his eyes for a moment, but turned and left mumbling. "I'm not the ex-con."

Keesha ran behind him and met him at the front door. Mark opened the door, stepped outside, and looked back at her. "Your father's a buster," he told her.

She really didn't want Mark to leave. She liked him a lot, but she also understood her father's frustration. "I'm sorry," she responded. "He's just stressed out."

Mark brushed it off. He looked over her shoulder. The coast was clear so he stole a quick kiss, touching his lips against hers and leaving it there for a few seconds. Keesha was stuck in the moment for a second, as he smiled and left. Feeling even more attracted to Mark's boldness, she smiled and went back into the living room.

Back in the living room, there was now mass hysteria. Everyone was talking at the same time.

"Mom, you use to be a nurse. You can help," Donteer gestured.

"Sure, get your mother involved," Leonard retorted.

"Everyone calm down!" April insisted.

"I don't know, Donteer," Mildred said, replying to her son's gesture.

Jamal was still looking at the man on the ground and noticed that he regained his consciousness, suddenly looking up at the new faces standing above him.

"Dad, he's moving," said Jamal, but neither Donteer nor anyone else heard the kid amidst the confusion.

Leonard was adamant in trying to get his point across to Donteer. "You shouldn't have brought him here," he said once again to Donteer.

"I heard you the first time, dad."

Sensing the pandemonium, the man attempted to speak.

"Thank . . ." he muttered.

But his voice was drowned by Mildred's. "Where is that ambulance?" she inquired. She then dialed emergency again.

Jamal, this time pulling his father's arm and trying once again to get his father's attention, spoke louder than everyone.

"Dad," he yelled over everyone else's voice.

"What?" Donteer snapped.

Jamal pointed to the man. They all looked at him together as he spoke from the ground.

"Thank . . . thank you."

* * *

"Yo pull over right there at that liquor store," Redd said to Brooklyn. "Let me get us something to drink."

As they drove down Linden Blvd., neither Brooklyn nor Redd thought about going to prison to do another bid; this time for the fourth time. They both had three strikes already as it was, and were both one foot out from being permanently discarded in some upstate prison somewhere. But they were thoughtless. Maybe their durags were too tight, or maybe they couldn't see that far because they both were slumped back in their seats, hardly even able to see over the dashboard. Or, maybe they couldn't hear over the rap rhythms that pumped through the speakers. Did somebody say Liquor?

Brooklyn pulled the station wagon over and Redd hopped out and went into the store. They were now in East New York. They'd split the money that they took from the man and were smoking weed and joy riding all night. This was their regular every Friday; find a victim, rob em, and spend the rest of the night getting wasted as if they didn't have a care in the world.

CHAPTER 8

Later on that night, everyone was exhausted and turned in to their rooms. Donteer, all cleaned up in a clean white tee shirt and sweat pants, stood in the doorway of the guest room.

In the room there was a chair, a dresser with a mirror, and a bed. Mildred stood over the man as he laid in the bed resting. His face was bruised, and his head wrapped in a clean bandage.

Mildred then turned and walked over to Donteer. "You get some rest too, he will be all right baby."

Donteer nodded his head. "I'm sorry for bringing him home mom. I just didn't know what else to do. Pedro at the store called for an ambulance first, but it didn't come."

"You could've took him inside Pedro store," Mildred said sternly. Then she thought for a second as she looked at the man all wrapped up in bandages. "But it's alright baby," she continued, patting Donteer's arm. "I know you were trying to do the right thing. And, truthfully, we can only do what the Lord asks of us." She paused, looked at the man lying in the bed, and continued. "He must've wanted you to do exactly what you did."

"Try telling dad that."

"I will. And I'm filing a complaint. I can't believe the EMS never showed up."

"It happens in a lot of hoods ma. I guess now it's happening in ours."

Mildred looked at her son dispirited, shook her head, and walked down the hall. Donteer stood there and looked at the man for a moment before he went downstairs in the basement where his son Jamal was.

* * *

In the basement, there was a washer and dryer off to the side. The dryer was on and Jamal was sitting on the washer in deep thought when Donteer walked in.

"Why are you sitting up there?" he asked Jamal.

With a guilty look on his face, Jamal jumped down and leaned against the washing machine. "I was just thinking dad."

"Did you put all those clothes in the machine like I said?"

"Yeah," Jamal responded. "They're finished washing. I put them in the dryer."

Donteer nodded. "So what are you thinking about?" he asked his son.

"Why granddad said those things to you . . . why you decided to be a hero tonight when you use to tell me don't be a hero be smart."

"I wasn't trying to be a hero son. I was doing what was right. But I would never do anything to put myself, or my family, in harm's way. There's a difference."

"I knew you'd say that dad."

Jamal was a very observant kid. He paid close attention to his dad. He listened closely to how Donteer treated his mom, to how he dealt with his grandparents, and to everyone he spoke to. But most of all, as he listened to his father, he listened to hear if Donteer was an honest man—a man worthy of his respect and obedience.

"Because it's the truth. And you have a good ear for the truth," said Donteer reassuringly with a smile.

Donteer knew that his son was at that age where he was beginning to make his own choices and decisions. And he tried his best with everything that he said and done to leave the best possible example for him. Especially with his prison record, Donteer thought it was imperative that counteracted this stigma in his son's eyes.

Jamal shook his head briskly, confirming that his father's words landed on good ground. "From your mouth to my ears dad."

"Yeah right," his dad said, still smiling.

Jamal attempted to walk past Donteer, but his father pulled him close and hugged him. "You've been hanging around the house a lot lately," he continued. "Don't think I haven't noticed. I know I've been busy, but we're gonna talk. Something's going on."

"I got it under control dad," Jamal stated, but Donteer already knew his son was going through something. They've always been close so Jamal knew he couldn't hide anything from his dad.

"I told you to get that kid Mark under control," Donteer replied, changing the topic. "I don't like him; he's too slick for your sister. I told you to keep him away from her."

They walked out of the room and into the hallway.

"Mom called me off," Jamal responded, while walking beside his dad.

"She did, huh? I'll talk to her."

❋ ❋ ❋

"Yo what's up with my money?" Tariq said aggressively as he approached Joker. Joker stood in front of Brooklyn's apartment building four blocks from Pedro's Deli. Besides the neighborhood park, this was the next hangout spot. Mostly everyone who were at the corner when Brooklyn and Redd had robbed the man were now relocated in front of Brooklyn's building.

Brooklyn's apartment building was on one of the hottest blocks in Brooklyn—Gates Ave. After hours, on any given night, this block was thick with hustlers, ballers, gangstas, and the wannabees. Every street image that a young boy or girl would want to become was out on the Ave. And, especially on a Friday night, luxury cars of all models lined the block all the way from Tompkins Ave. to Marcus Garvey Blvd. Some cruised slowly down the block making their presence felt. Others stopped while their rims kept spinning. Still others pull up against the curb, hopped out and profiled.

This was Stuntin 101 to its fullest. And the women loved it. Music blasted everywhere, while strobe lights flashed. But Tariq was all too use to this scene. Actually he grew tired of it. To him, most of these dudes didn't put no work in in the streets the way he did. They didn't hustle from sun-up to sun-down the way he hustled. They loved the shine but not the grind. And all this scene did was make Tariq wanna rob one of these fools.

But of course he wouldn't. For one, they all knew him or knew of him. And two, he was a patient hustler and cognizant of his surroundings. Unlike Brooklyn and Redd he knew that you never rob someone in the same hood where you live and where your family live, or sooner or later it'll come back to haunt you. He'd rather take his time, grinding day and night, and hustle his way to the top.

As Tariq made his way up Gates Ave, about an hour after the incident took place on the corner, he acknowledged all whom he deemed worthy of his head-nod in route to Brooklyn's building. He had already went home, changed his clothes and slung on his diamond encrusted white gold chain over his fresh white tee shirt. And as always he was feeling himself. He wasn't the flambuoyant type, he was just trying to switch up his image in order to blend in on the Ave. He especially didn't want to be linked to no robbery so he switched up. It was as he approached the mob in front of Brooklyn's building that he noticed Joker and began to press him about his money. "I been looking for you," Tariq told him as he approached. "I thought you said you was gonna see me with my money last month."

Tariq just loved making a scene, especially when it concerned his money. He would see to it that all who was around listening would not make the same mistake as Joker did.

"I was looking for you," Joker responded, quickly digging into his pocket and pulling out five twenty dollar bills and holding it out to Tariq. "This is all I got right now."

Tariq was about to take the money but hesitated when Joker said it was all he had. He knew that Joker wasn't looking for him. If he was he would've found him. He didn't have a problem finding him when he wanted the product, Tariq thought. "Homie, if I check your pockets right now and you have any more money, I'ma punch you in your face for lying to me."

Everyone called him Joker because he was always cracking jokes on everybody, but it wasn't nothing funny about what Tariq said to him. Joker knew Tariq wasn't playing but he honestly didn't have any more money. Truth was, he had two hundred dollars, but spent half of it on more weed that very same night. He didn't expect to see Tariq. "Ta, I wouldn't lie to you," he responded, quickly pulling out his own pockets. "You've always looked out for me. It's all I have, but I'ma have the rest for you over the weekend."

Tariq stared at him for a few seconds then took the cash out of his hand. "If I don't get the rest of my money by Sunday, I better not see you no more."

Just then as he said this an unmarked police car rode by slowly, observing all the faces that were in front of the building. Tariq and Joker both made eye contact with the cops as they rode by. Tariq then put the money into his pocket and crossed the street going into the building directly adjacent from Brooklyn's. Joker went inside the building and everyone else carried on, totally unmoved by the unmarked car that disappeared down the block.

CHAPTER 9

In Donteer's parent's room, Leonard was sitting up in the bed when Mildred climbed into it with her pajamas on. She picked up her Bible from off the night table, and opened it up to the Gospel of Matthew. Mildred made it a habit to read some Scriptures, most times out loud for Leonard to hear, before she went to sleep. She had plans on starting the Beatitudes but decided to speak to her husband first about what had taken place earlier.

"You shouldn't have spoken to Donteer that way in front of the kids," Mildred begun.

"I was upset," Leonard responded, still visibly upset.

"Yeah, but still you don't undermine your son like that. It'll make the children think less of him."

"The kids respect him. He's not respecting us, bringing a stranger into our home. He could've prompted those muggers to follow him here. Then what?"

"Leonard please!"

Mildred had no intentions for the conversation to go off into an argument. She was tired, but it was obvious that Leonard was just getting started. "Yeah, no one wants to talk about the negative stuff that could've happened," he continued.

"Everything is fine," Mildred stated. "The man will recover."

"We know that now, but Donteer had no way of knowing that before he brought him into our home. That's all I'm saying."

Mildred was sure she wasn't gonna go a minute further into this discussion. Her husband can really be unreasonable sometimes, she thought. But she got her point across. She put her Bible back down, reached over and turned off the lamp. "Well you've said it," she concluded. "Now can I get some sleep?" She then laid down.

Leonard sat up for a few more seconds then laid down also, turning away from his wife.

❋ ❋ ❋

Donteer and April's bedroom was lit up in earth tones. There was a big chart with the heading 'April's Showers,' on the side. It was a diagram of April's fight with cancer. It included relevant dates; diagnosis and treatment dates, and the day she stopped praying. This was about a year before Donteer came out of prison.

In the room was also a bed, a dresser, a bathroom on the side, and a vanity table. April was sitting before the table in a chair looking in the mirror, which was attached to the table, when Donteer entered the room, walked over, and stood behind her.

"Are you all right baby?" he asked her with a concerned look on his face.

She continued to stare into the mirror at her face, which looked ashen. "Do I look pallid?" she asked, without even looking up at him.

Donteer leaned over his wife's shoulder from behind and hugged her. "You look fine, hon," he said smiling.

"Well I don't feel fine."

April began to cry. The cancer had really broken her down, emotionally more than anything. A lone tear rolled down her cheek, then another. "I feel like some of my radiance is gone." She sniffled. "I'm scared, Don."

Donteer felt everything his wife was going through as if he was going through it with her. He loved her with his very life but he knew he had to be strong for her. Besides, his faith in Jesus was growing. "Don't be," he reaffirmed her. "It'll be all right."

"I don't want to go through that treatment again."

Donteer was still hugging her from behind the chair when she shook herself loose and got up. He let her go and stood back as she vented some more.

"And I don't need the stress right now, Donteer."

"I'm not trying to stress you hon."

"You're not?" she responded indignantly. "Then why bring an injured man home, yelling and screaming, scaring everybody."

"He needed help," Donteer stated.

"I need help. You need employment help. Your family needs help. Keesha is at that age where she's very self-conscious about everything. Why don't you help around here before you go into the street spreading benevolence?"

Donteer looked dejected.

"That's not fair April, I'm here for my family." April walked over and sat on the bed while Donteer followed her. "I'm here for Keesha. I know she is self-conscious about her weight. That fast boy Mark knows it too. That's why he's sniffing around her."

"Oh Donteer, she likes the boy. That's why I let him come over here, so I can supervise them."

"But you can't be around them all the time. That's why I put Jamal on him."

"No one can be around Keesha all the time. She's smart; she's not gonna do anything stupid. And Jamal has his own life to live."

"I don't want that boy around here," Donteer stated firmly. "He's promiscuous."

"Donteer, they're only fifteen. Next year when they're Jamal's age we'll worry about warding off promiscuity."

"Next year might be . . ."

April cut him off then flared up and began crying again. "Not now Donteer! Please, I have to go visit Sheila tomorrow. She's terminal. And I have to go for my follow up test Tuesday. I'm not in the mood."

"Okay, okay, baby, we'll talk about this later," said Donteer as he walked toward the room door.

Dealing with April's mood swings were sometimes hard for Donteer. She had given up hope. It was like she hated herself. She'd literally let herself go mentally after being diagnosed with cancer. And, as a result, everything else followed. Her mind became unstable and her emotions uncontrollable. She almost seemed bi-polar. "You're still taking me over to her place, right?" She asked him.

"Yes," he responded solemnly as he thought about their friend Sheila. Cancer just came out of nowhere and robbed them of their childhood friend. In a matter of a year after being diagnosed, it took over her body. And now it was trying to take his wife hostage.

"Well, we have to get there early because her relatives usually visit her on Saturday afternoons." April added, snapping him back to reality.

"Okay," Donteer responded. "God help us all," he added, as he looked back into his wife's eyes.

Afterwards, he left the room and peeked into his son's room, who was sleeping.

❋ ❋ ❋

In Keesha's room, which was a typical teenage girl's room, there were posters on the wall of rap stars. There was also a bed, a table with a make-up counter, and a large mirror. Keesha was laying on the bed talking on the phone to her friend Kim.

"Kim," Keesha said to her, "I'm not trying to get into that he say she say stuff."

Kim was very cute and popular, but she was brutally honest. So much so, that Keesha cringed whenever Kim had some any news to tell her.

"So you don't want to know what Mark's friends said about you?" she asked Keesha.

"No," Keesha answered.

"Okay."

"All right," Keesha recanted. "What did they say?"

"That you were cute, but fat," said Kim immediately.

"I don't care!"

"One of them calls you the pork wagon," Kim continued.

"His mother!" Keesha shot back.

Donteer peeked his head into his daughter's room just in time to hear her last outburst.

"Whose mother?" he asked her. Keesha attempted to conceal the phone as he walked into the room. "And who are you talking to on that phone?" he continued. "It better not be that boy Mark!"

Keesha sucked her teeth. "It's Kim, and this is my private space daddy. You should knock first."

Donteer walked closer to her. "Me and you don't have anything private," he told her, motioning for the phone which she gave him. "Hello?" he said into the phone.

"Hi, Mr. Brown," Kim answered.

"Kim, it's late. Say good night to Keesha. I'm sure you two will be seeing each other over the weekend."

Donteer handed the phone back to his daughter so she can say good night.

"Yeah, I'll see you tomorrow." Keesha hung up and handed it back to Donteer, who had his hand out stretched. He put it down on a nearby dresser.

"So what got you all excited?" he asked her.

"Some boy said something that wasn't too flattering about me."

"People love to put other people down," he said immediately, "only because they're insecure about something. You heard your grandfather's tirade tonight." Knowing how his daughter was very self-conscious because she was overweight, Donteer used every opportunity to prepare her for a world that was brutal, especially to those who cared so much about people think. "People talk about my having been in prison. Do you think I let them keep me down? I'm not perfect."

"Nobody is!" Keesha said without looking at him.

"That's right. I didn't want to go to prison but being there may have saved my life. Being an alumnus of the school of hard knocks puts me in some very good company. Jesus was a prisoner."

Keesha cracked a smile. She was still visibly hurt, and really didn't feel like talking but Donteer always had a way of breaking through her tough shell. She thought it amusing to hear him talk about Jesus.

"And you know what I always say about Jesus, right?" he continued.

She responded, but still with a slight attitude. "They talked about Him, so expect folks to talk about us."

"There it is," he added smiling.

Donteer also tried to encourage her to be bold, especially in her faith in the Lord.

"It's easy for you to say dad, you don't have as many friends as I do." Donteer looked amusingly shocked. He knew she was hurt and this was her way of covering it up. "I mean immature friends. I'm in a High School. Looks, and what people think, matter."

"It doesn't have to baby. It's really never about what anyone thinks or says about you. It's about how you see yourself."

Keesha looked like she was about to cry.

"I'm not that confident yet daddy," she said, as a lone tear slowly rolled down her cheek. Donteer hugged her briefly.

"I know baby," he said as he released her, looking into her eyes. "I wasn't either at your age. Most people aren't. But you will be." Donteer then stood up. "Get some rest baby," he told her, kissing her forehead. She settled into her bed and he reached over to cut off the lamp, but paused. "Remember, you're unique, baby, because all of God's daughters are glorious within."

He cut the light off and went into the guest room where the man was.

❋ ❋ ❋

"I don't know why you came over here in the first place," Tiffany said to Tariq, as she put on her clothes. "I'm going out."

Tiffany was one of Tariq's three kids' mothers. She lived in the building across the street from Brooklyn's building. Of his three kids' mothers, she was the only one who condoned his lifestyle and it was because she was the female version of him, always running the streets and neglecting their son. Tariq was high, slouched in her couch and watching television. He was trying to block her out as she rambled on about him not giving her money in a while for their son Anthony. And because he ignored her, she tried to get him to leave.

"Tiffany, I don't care about you going out with your lil boyfriend. I came to see my son."

"I told you he's asleep, and Lisa's on her way over here to watch him. We saw when your little friends robbed that guy on the corner, so knowing you, you're probably just trying to lay low right now. Tariq, I don't have time for this. I gotta go."

Deep down, Tiffany was tired of Tariq's games, just wasting his life . . . and hers. At one time, just after giving birth to Anthony she did hope that he would change and settle down with her, but she soon gave up hope. She saw that his heart was in the streets. She still loved his crazy behind though. But she was beginning to realize that her feelings for him was costing her too much. And she had determined that she had to get out and live her own life, or it would slip her by.

Of course Tiffany had no problem getting the attention she thought she deserved. In fact, at six feet tall, her tawny, brown skin and voluptuousness commanded all attention from men of all breeds and types. From the moment she stepped foot out of or into anywhere, all eyes gave in to her. And she was addicted to the attention. Most weekends she was either at some club or out on a date. That night, Macko, a big-time baller was on his way over to take her out.

But Tariq had his mind bent on staying at her place. Being directly across the street from Brooklyn's apartment building, he could see directly in front of Brooklyn's building from her bedroom window. And he wanted to see Brooklyn early the next morning before he left. Besides, Tariq already knew that Tiffany loved him and would do anything for him. He also knew that she really wanted him to stay with her that night by the way she moved in and out of the room while she spoke with him; as if after seeing him looking all good, she was now confused about the plans that she had. And, just as Tariq would have it, Tiffany cancelled all her plans for him that night.

The hood is crazy like that sometimes. For those trying to move upward, forward, move on, or just move, there's always an invisible, unrelenting and downward pull to nowhere. And taking control of one's life seems twice as hard than for others in society at large.

Unbeknownst to Tariq, and other young men like himself, he contributed to this matrix. Because of his lust for money and power, others who were drawn to his influence, like Brooklyn, Redd, and all the Lil homies, were drawn into this darkness. They then became stuck, mentally and unable to move; stuck in a rut of emotions like Tiffany. And soon, without divine intervention, his son Anthony would end up like him, or even worse than Tariq could ever dream to be.

CHAPTER 10

The light was dim, and the man was now resting. His eyes were closed when Donteer entered the room and took a seat in a chair across from the bed. Donteer bowed his head, praying silently, and when he opened his eyes the man was staring at him faintly.

"Prayer is good for the soul," he said with his eyes still not fully opened. He almost startled Donteer.

"I . . . know," Donteer responded hesitantly. "How do you feel?"

"Battered and bruised, but better," he said, struggling somewhat to talk.

"I'll take that to mean that you'll pull through."

"I'll make it," he replied confidently.

"I was a little worried," Donteer continued. "You suffered a bad lump to the head. Luckily my mother was a nurse. She helped clean you up."

The man then looked down at the clothes he had on. "They didn't take my clothes too, did they?"

"We removed them so they could be washed."

"Thanks a lot," the man responded. "But I'll need them back."

Donteer smiled. “Trust me,” he told him. “We wouldn’t dream of keeping them. And that tee-shirt you had on under your dress shirt with the word ‘DOG’ on it isn’t very fashionable.”

The man returned the smile. “I like to wear that when I frequent rough neighborhoods.”

“Like this one?”

“I’ve visited worse. Are you the person that helped me?” the man inquired. “Because several didn’t, you know.”

“I heard. And yes, it was me.” Donteer told him. “This is my home you’re in. I brought you here because the ambulance didn’t come. And I didn’t know what else to do.”

“Thanks again. That was mighty Christian of you.”

“How do you know I’m Christian?” Donteer asked him.

“I can tell . . . and I observed you praying,” he answered.

Donteer nodded his head in agreement, but remained silent. Then the man continued to acquaint himself. “How long have you been a Christian?” he asked Donteer.

“A couple of years,” said Donteer. “I was born again while I was in prison.”

“That’s a good thing. Better then than never. How long did you do?” the man probed.

“Thirty-six months. But I don’t like to talk too much about that.”

“Ashamed?”

“Somewhat,” Donteer responded, “but also because I don’t like to dwell on the past. It prevents me from seeing the future clearly.”

Seeing that Donteer didn’t want to go there, the man changed the topic. “Why’d you help me?” he asked.

“Truthfully, I don’t know,” Donteer answered. “It all happened very quickly. I mean, I don’t know you.”

"The name is Abler Pen."

Donteer looked curious.

"It fits me well," Abler continued, speaking of his name. "In my spare time I scribe. Only, my work goes beyond paper into real life situations. Sorta like writing a book of life."

"You that good, huh?"

"That's what they say," Abler responded. "You're supposed to introduce yourself after someone introduces themself."

"Oh, excuse me. I'm Donteer Brown. This is my family's home. My wife April, my son Jamal, daughter Keesha, and my parents, Leonard and Mildred, all live here."

"Sounds like you have a beautiful Christian family," Abler continued.

Donteer smiled.

"Thank you," he responded. "Everyone embraces the Christian faith, except for my father. He does, but not out loud, or in deed."

"Good for ya'll, bad for him. But prayer, and patience can fix that."

"I feel like I know you."

"Is that why you helped me?"

"No, because I don't know you."

Abler smiled confidently. "But you feel like you do?" Still smiling, he gazed into Donteer's eyes. "Maybe you helped me because the Spirit moved you to do so."

Donteer laughed in amusement. "I don't think so," he responded. "I told you, I'm new to this Christian stuff. Most Christians don't even accept me."

"Do you want to talk about that?"

Donteer looked curious once again. "Not really," he said. Then he got a bit more serious. "Why were you around here? Where do you live?"

Donteer was skeptical, and rightly so. This was still a stranger in his home with his family, he thought. And he was still living in the hood. He felt as though he was getting way too comfortable. Abler noticed this and decided to reveal a bit more about himself.

"I'm new to these parts. I don't have lodging yet, but I do have a job. I work for a delivery company called Heaven Sent."

"You're a messenger?" asked Donteer.

"At your service. Ahh . . ."

Abler grimaced in pain, as Donteer got up and moved closer to the bed.

"Are you all right?" Donteer asked him after a few seconds, genuinely concerned.

Abler sighed and closed his eyes momentarily, then he opened it up slowly. "The pain shot straight up into my head," he said. "I got a little dizzy also. Some aftershocks I think. I can't get too excited."

"No you can't. You're technically still in recovery."

"Can you get me some water, please?" Abler requested. "My throat suddenly feels a little parched."

"Sure," Donteer said. He turned and headed for the door. Then he stopped, looked back at Abler who closed his eyes. Donteer turned back around, hurrying out. "Be right back," he said.

* * *

In the kitchen, Donteer opened the cabinet and took a cup. He filled it with some water from the faucet, but thought for a moment. He thought it was unhospitable to offer a house guest faucet water. He then turned the faucet off, took a bottled water from the refrigerator and went back in the room with Abler.

❋ ❋ ❋

"Can you help me sit up?" Abler asked just as Donteer walked back into the guest room and over to the bed.

"Yeah," Donteer obliged, hurrying over to him.

Donteer put the bottled water and cup down at the bedside. He then sat Abler upright, placing a pillow behind him to support his back. He turned and got the water, opened the bottle, poured some into the cup, and handed Abler the cup.

Abler drank a good amount of the water, handed it back to Donteer, and made a another request. "I really hope I'm not asking too much of you," he said, "but could you do one more thing for me?"

"What's that?"

"Could you pour a little bit of that water out of the window?"

Donteer looked confused. "What for?" he asked.

"For the both of us."

"I don't understand."

"We're humbling ourselves before God. Water poured on the ground is a symbol of human weaknesses and limitations."

This was sort of strange to Donteer. I've heard of pour out a little liquor for the dead homies, he thought. But pour out a little water . . .

Hesitantly, however, he went over to the window, opened it, and poured some water out of the bottle. He then closed the window and took a seat in the chair. "You're very religious?" Donteer then asked Abler.

"Religious no," Abler asserted, "spiritual yes. Religious is outward to show others, being spiritual is within, for God."

"So you're a Christian?" Donteer inquired.

"Completely!"

"And a messenger?" Donteer continued. "You were telling me that you're homeless?"

"Not homeless, just without home for now. It's like when someone isn't physically in the Lord's house, but understands that they *are* His house. I don't have a home, but I'm comfortable wherever I go because I know that His presence is with me, and in me."

"You work for a delivery company?" Donteer probed.

"Heaven Sent! We're very much into servicing communities like these."

"You can get hurt, or even killed, helping in some communities," Donteer stated.

"Yet you did just that and you're still alive talking to me."

"I'm a different type of breed."

Donteer and Abler both smiled.

"Call it what you want," Abler maintained. "In my book you're a Good Samaritan. This world needs more of your breed."

"I appreciated the accolade but I'll prefer a job though." Donteer smiled good-humoredly, but he was serious. "Are they hiring at your company?" he asked.

"We seek out messengers periodically," Abler responded. "I'll keep you in mind if a position opens up."

"I'm just talking. I'm really trying to get into the business sector."

"Corporate?"

"I wish," Donteer said smiling.

"Praying is better than wishing."

"I pray. Earlier I said a prayer for your quick recovery."

"And I'm feeling better already. You need to keep praying because the Lord's answering."

"What type of transportation do you use?" asked Donteer. "A bike?"

"A station wagon. It's my work vehicle, and they took it."

Donteer appeared concerned. "What else did they take?" he inquired further.

"That, and all the packages I'm to deliver. They were in the back seat. The letters and telegrams were in the glove compartment."

"Is everything replaceable?"

"I'm afraid not," Abler answered. "Like I said before, our services extend into many communities, mostly Christians. And I'm also on a very strict schedule. This can really set me back."

"You make it sound grave," said Donteer.

"That's because it is, Donteer. Everyone's service is important to someone, or it wouldn't be an occupation. Just happens that I take mines very serious."

"Then maybe we should call the police," Donteer suggested.

"The criminal mind is an irrational one," Abler responded. "If we do that, those responsible for this theft will destroy all evidence of it. If they do that, we will not be better off than we are now."

"What's in the packages?"

"That I can't tell you. I will say this, everything being delivered is significant to those receiving them." Abler laid back down on the bed after saying this. He closed his eyes then fell asleep while Donteer stared out of the window deep in thought. He realized that Abler was in a deeper predicament than he thought. And in a weird way he felt responsible. After all, he did know the knuckleheads who committed this atrocity.

❋ ❋ ❋

Early the next morning, the sunlight beamed through the guest room window into Abler's face. His bruises were clearly visible as he laid in the bed asleep. Donteer was also asleep. They both woke simultaneously, but Abler spoke first. "You sat in here and watched me all night?" He asked Donteer.

"You're still a stranger in my house," Donteer responded. "I'm faithful, not stupid," he added.

Abler found this hilarious, but just chuckled. "I promise you, I do not pose a threat. I'm truly grateful."

"How do you feel?" Donteer asked him.

"I have a terrible headache. My stomach is queasy. And I don't think my legs will support me."

"That good, huh? Do you have any friends or relatives that I could call?" inquired Donteer.

"I have no family or friends in these parts."

"Well I can let you stay for a while, but we have to get you on your way soon."

"I need to continue with my charge," Abler added. "Can you help me?"

"I don't know if I can get your stuff back. Honestly, I really doubt it."

"I'll appreciate your help. The rest, I'll leave up to the Lord."

Donteer nodded. "We'll see what happens."

CHAPTER 11

The morning was a bright and balmy one. April leaned her head against the headrest, thinking and admiring the pedestrians who walked down Fulton Street. Donteer's eyelids were heavy from a long and exhausting night and not enough sleep. They were on their way to Park Slope to see their friend, Sheila. As they stood at the traffic light waiting for it to turn green he reached over and clasped April's hand as she continued looking out of the car window.

Donteer knew that it was those silent moments that lured April to contemplate too much about her situation, especially being that she was going to see her once vibrant and beautiful friend. So he spoke casually, if for no other reason, to take her mind off of her predicament. "He seems like a trustworthy person," Donteer stated, "very faithful. He's still a bit broken up though. I asked mom to allow him to stay the weekend. And I told Jamal to watch him."

"You act like Jamal's a security guard," April responded somewhat annoyed. "Stop telling that boy to watch people. You need to watch the people he's hanging out with," she added.

"I'm watching April. I know all about those little roughnecks from up the block that be calling for him. He doesn't hang out with them so it's not smart to say anything yet."

"Why not?"

"You know, see how it plays out. Jamal's a strong kid. We have to give him a chance to stand on his own. This is how you let boys become men. If he needs me, then I'll be there."

A few minutes later Donteer pulled the car over directly in front of Sheila's house and parked. April immediately started feeling queasy. Looking at how Sheila deteriorated only reminded her of the fate of so many women in their position. Most of all, she saw herself in Sheila's face.

When they knocked on the door, Sheila answered. She had on an old house coat, which seemed to swallow her up, with a scarf covering her bald head. Her eyes were sunken, and her face ashen. April felt a knot in her throat as she tried to greet her old friend, but somehow was able to force a word out. "Hey," she greeted Sheila.

Sheila hugged her, then she hugged Donteer as he greeted her also. "Hi Sheila," he said smiling.

She ushered them into her elegantly furnished living room. "Come in ya'll."

❋ ❋ ❋

"How's it going, Sheila?" April asked, as they sat side by side on a sofa in Sheila's living room. Donteer sat quietly across from the women. April held Sheila's hand, patting it, while she spoke to her.

"Slow," she answered. "That's really the worst part. How are you?"

"Better," April responded. She was lying. Since she was diagnosed, her life just seemed to disintegrate.

Sheila had always been like a big sister to April. That's why it hurt April so much watching cancer take its toll and she was unable to help. Cancer is very cadaverous, April thought. Even as she sat there speaking to Sheila, lumps were again beginning to form in her own throat.

"Did you have your follow-up yet?" Sheila asked her.

"Tuesday," April answered. Trying to remain strong is all she could've done now but she was terrified. What did she do to deserve such a thing? What did they do? Her friend Sheila had always been such a blessing in her life, especially during Donteer's incarceration. She supported April emotionally all the times she was lonely and didn't have anyone to talk to. If there was anyone who April thought was strong it was Sheila. This is why it hurted so bad the more she thought about their predicament.

"You'll be okay," Sheila tried to reaffirm her, as a lone tear slipped from April's eye. "April, stop that."

"I know, I'm sorry," April responded, now finding it hard to even look at Sheila's face.

"It's okay," Sheila reaffirmed her. "My Father is calling me home. And I'm ready to go give my report."

April nodded as Donteer looked at the women dismally.

"I had a wonderful life. It was short—forty years—but full years, with good friends," Sheila added.

Sheila then hugged April. When they separated, Sheila looked over at Donteer. "Take care of my friend, Donteer. She's got a whole lotta life left in her."

"I will," Donteer said reassuringly, with a half-smile on his face.

"I wish I would have married, and not taken the institution for granted."

April interjected. "Sheila, don't go there."

"No, it's okay. I'm just thinking out loud. I see what you and Donteer have, and it's special. I've known so since the two of you were childhood sweethearts." April smiled at Sheila, then glanced at Donteer before Sheila continued. "And I never faulted you Donteer for the incident that sent you to prison. That man should have never tried to grab April."

April really didn't want to go back through that incident. She hated dwelling on it. If it wasn't for that, she often thought, she would've never been in the predicament she was. "Sheila, we don't need to go there."

"No, I need to tell Donteer this," she objected. She then looked Donteer squarely in his eyes. "I know the courts convicted you of attempted murder, but in my eyes you were justified."

At least someone understood, Donteer thought. Even though he knew he was wrong for letting his temper get the best of him, deep down he still felt somewhat justified in trying to protect his wife. So what he went a little too far. To him it was warranted. After all, he always asked himself, what would've happened if he didn't break away from Tariq when he did? April could've really gotten hurt. Sheila really made him feel better and at peace, because all the dirty looks he got in church made him feel more guilty than he was.

"I appreciate that, Sheila. But honestly I did take it too far. I've come to terms with myself and the incident. He was wrong. He violated my baby, but I was wrong as well. And I'm thankful that he didn't die."

"I'm too tired to argue anymore." She struggled to laugh. "I just agree to disagree."

Sheila then turned to April and touched her cheek. "You have to start praying again," she told her little sister. "Donteer wants you to, and so do I."

April looked at Donteer quickly before turning back to Sheila. "You two have been talking behind my back."

"Forget all that. Pray through it girl."

April had gave Jesus an honest try. She went to church and prayed tirelessly, without ceasing, just as her friend Sheila did. But to no avail. She kept her feelings subdued, however, but being around Sheila and seeing how quickly she deteriorated made her realize just how forsaken she felt. "It didn't do you any good," she told Sheila. "Or me."

"No, it did," Sheila told April. "I was wrong. Just because our prayers aren't always answered when and how we like them to be, doesn't mean that God hasn't heard them."

"You're praying again now, even though you've stopped treatment?"

"Yes, oh yes! And it's given me a peace that I can't explain. My spirit is so free April. Cancer may be able to separate me from this earth, but it can't separate me from God."

❋ ❋ ❋

"I told ya'll dudes about making me hot," Tariq scolded Brooklyn, as they stood in the staircase of Brooklyn's mom's apartment building. Tariq did have a couple guys selling weed on the corner for him, but he could care less about being hot. He just wanted to know what Brooklyn and Redd got from their heist. "I hope it was worth it cause now I can't get no money on the corner for at least a couple weeks."

"Yo Ta, that dude was looking mad sweet with that knot in his hand," Brooklyn responded with a smile on his face. "I had to get em."

Tariq cracked a smile as he heard about the knot. He was up all night wondering about what they came off with. That's why he got up bright and early that Saturday morning to check Brooklyn before he went on a wild spending spree. To him, neither Brooklyn nor Redd were capable of managing anything and they needed his help. "Ya'll dudes is crazy," he continued. "What you get?" he finally asked.

"Yo you wouldn't believe this. He had close to two gs." Brooklyn pulled his portion of the two thousand dollars from out of his pocket as Tariq's eyes grew wide. "Dude must've just came from the bank cause these bills are so crispy," he said smiling. Then he put the money back in his pocket. "I broke Redd off already. He should be coming over here soon."

Brooklyn and Redd's joyride ended off at Redd's uncle's house, where Redd lived. His uncle Ricky wore a semblance of the rapper Rick Ross . . . an older smoked-out version. Not that older if you asked him though. Since, in his mind, forty was the new thirty, then he was still only about forty years old. He was Redd's mother youngest brother.

Uncle Ricky had always been a hustler, from as far back as Redd can remember. Back in his days he was an OG for real. Being that Redd never knew his father and didn't care to know any of his mother's boyfriends, he gravitated to the closest person he had as a father figure—Uncle Ricky. And being that his mother was so caught up with all the men that came in and out of her life, she happily obliged when Redd asked her to live with his uncle since the age of fifteen.

Fifteen years later, and all that Redd had to show for his years of being groomed under his favorite uncle was how to cook, bag, and sell crack. This was how he hooked up with Brooklyn. Redd's uncle Ricky, who sold small quantities of weight at the time, became Brooklyn and Tariq's drug connect until he fell off. That's because he started smoking his own product. However, even though he himself wasn't resourceful to Tariq, Uncle Ricky still had his old connects. And Tariq told Brooklyn to keep Redd close because they may need a plug or connect from Uncle Ricky.

"Redd gotta holla at us about some spot out in PA." Brooklyn told Tariq, still standing in the staircase. "This may be our come-up Ta. Uncle Ricky said that they quadrupling their money out there. He got some peoples out there that's ready to set up shop with us."

"If they making all that money, and they got their own spots and all that, then why they need us?"

"There's a drought out there," Brooklyn continued. "No drugs. They need a constant flow of drugs to get the town poppin. All we gotta do is get it out there," he added. "I think it's Wilkes Barre, Pennyslvania. Yo homie, I feel real good about this."

"I don't know about no outta of town moves right now champ," Tariq said. "Who gonna keep things together out here?"

Tariq knew of far too many dudes trying to blow up the fast way by going out of town, only to never come back alive. Either they'd be murdered by the out-of-towners, or robbed, kidnapped, or snitched on, and then put away in some out of town jail somewhere where they knew no one and no one knew them. "I gotta think about that," Tariq added. He knew that if he was going to make a move like that he would have to thoroughly weigh his options, considering the pros and cons first. He'd have to be ready to lay down all who opposed them. And he'd have to be sure that the money was well worth it. "We gotta get some paper if we're gonna make any move and right now our money's funny." Tariq decided to leave it at that for the time being. "Where Redd at?" he asked Brooklyn.

"He had to make a couple runs for Uncle Ricky. He said he'll be here by noon and fill us in on all the details."

"And where's the car?"

"In Uncle Ricky's garage.

"That's what's up!" Tariq said enthusiastically. "Let's hit the gambling spot while the corner cools off and make that money make money for us."

CHAPTER 12

"You look better than you did last night," Jamal told Abler, as he stood before him in the guest room.

Abler was now sitting up in the bed. He was dressed in his slacks, shoes, and his tee shirt that said DOG across his chest. His face was bruised, and his head was still bandaged all the way around. He couldn't help but to smile at Jamal's comment. "I'll take that as a compliment," he responded.

He then stood up and looked himself in the mirror as Jamal studied him.

"That's a nice shirt," Jamal complimented him again.

"At least somebody recognize, thank you Jamal."

"You're welcome. My dad told me that you wear it to blend in. But you're not really hood."

"Your dad's right. I'm not." Abler smiled. "I'm more . . . eternal."

"I know a guy named Eternal."

Abler tried to laugh, then a grimace crossed his face. Jamal noticed his reaction. "It still hurts huh?" he asked him.

"A little," Abler responded, still visibly in pain.

"Maybe you should lay back down," Jamal then suggested.

"No!" Abler asserted, his expression changing. "I think I should move around and get my body to rebound. Can I see your room?" he asked Jamal.

Jamal was a little surprised that Abler would want to see his room, but it wasn't a problem. "I guess so," he consented. "Come on."

❋ ❋ ❋

When they came into Jamal's room, the first thing Abler noticed was the various posters of basketball and football athletes. "You like sports?" He asked Jamal.

"Yeah. Hey, what kind of name is Abler?"

"My father gave me the name because he said I was superbly capable and talented."

"Oh, that's cool," Jamal responded excited.

While they were talking, Jamal heard someone call him from the outside, and he jumped as though he was scared. It was Biz from down the block. Jamal tried to stay clear of him and his sidekick, Pooh. But it seemed as though the more he tried to stay away from them, they came looking for him.

"Hey Jamal, come downstairs!" Biz shouted from outside the window. Abler noticed Jamal's hesitation.

"What's wrong?" Abler asked Jamal.

"That's Biz. He's this kid from down the block that keeps sweating me. He wants me to hang out with him."

"But you don't want to?"

"Not really, Biz is sort of a trouble maker."

Abler went to peek out the window and saw Biz and Pooh. "There are two of them."

"The other guy is his road dawg, Pooh. They're always together."

"You gonna go downstairs?" Abler asked him.

"Yeah, if I don't, Biz will think I'm ducking him."

"But you are," responded Abler.

"I don't want him to know that."

"I'll go with you," Abler then offered, which caught Jamal by surprise.

Jamal never told anyone about his fear of Biz. He kept it to himself because he was embarrassed. Also because telling the wrong person can make it worse, he thought. Biz and Pooh would tell everyone that he was scared, and that he told on them. But it was something about Abler's request that made him feel comfortable.

"Do you have a hat I can borrow?" he asked Jamal confidently.

Abler was serious, and confident. And it gave Jamal a sense of courage.

❋ ❋ ❋

"I want you to pray for me before you leave," Sheila told April, still sitting side by side. It was time for April and Donteer to leave and, as usual, April was going to be the first one to start crying. Each time before leaving Sheila's, April felt worse because each time she thought it would be her last time seeing her big sister. So before April sprang her fountain, Sheila asked April to pray for her, trying also to encourage her to start back praying.

"I'm at that place that only the Lord can heal me, and only through prayers He's gonna do so," she said, smiling at April. "And who else better to pray for me than my little sister, who feels my pain. And April, please don't pray no weak prayer. I need His power. Pray for me like you were praying for yourself . . . like your life depended on it."

Both April and Donteer smiled. Donteer got up and went over to where the women sat, sitting on the other side of Sheila and reached out his hands for both of their hands. April hesitated for a moment, took a deep breath, waiting for her thoughts to gather, and for the first time in a long time, she truly prayed, believing that her words went from her lips to God's ear.

CHAPTER 13

Abler and Jamal exited the house together. Abler had a black skull hat over his bandaged head. Biz and Pooh were standing on the sidewalk in front of the neighbor's house.

"You want me to walk over with you?" Abler requested.

"Nah, I'ma just go see what he wants."

Jamal walked over to where Biz and Pooh were standing while Abler stood on the porch looking at all three of them.

Biz was standing there looking at Jamal as he approached. Pooh looked at Abler, then he turned around and began looking up the block in the opposite direction. Biz seemed anxious to speak to Jamal. "What's up Jamal?" he said smiling.

"Nothing," Jamal answered nonchalantly.

Biz looked over at Abler. "Who's that?"

Jamal looked back at Abler then turned back to Biz. "A friend of my father's."

"What's he looking at, you or me?" Biz asked Jamal, still looking at Abler.

"Nah, he just stepped out to get some air."

Pooh stood next to Biz, just staring hard at Jamal as they both now focused their attention on him. Pooh was anxious to make his presence felt. "You don't see anyone else standing here?" he asked Jamal.

"I see you Pooh," Jamal responded, now looking at him.

"So why didn't you speak to me?"

Jamal shrugged his shoulders as if to say, "I don't know."

Biz then took control. "Yo chill out, Jamal is a friend of ours. Right Jamal?"

Jamal shook his head in agreement, but reluctantly. "Yeah," he responded.

Pooh laughed, and walked a couple steps away, closer to Abler, and stared at him. But Abler was unmoved, and met Pooh's eyes with pierces of his own. Pooh then turned and walked back to them chuckling, as Biz pressed Jamal.

Biz moved closer to the side of Jamal's face and spoke to him. Each word was simultaneous with each poke of the finger, and spoken with emphasis. "We-better-be-friends-Jamal-because-you-don't-want-me-as-an-enemy," Biz said, making sure that Jamal understood fully what he was saying.

Jamal folded up, nodding his head and listening to his words as Pooh walked back over and stood beside Biz, looking at Jamal. Pooh was a little shook up by Abler's presence.

"Man, let's get out of here," he said. "That dude on the porch is creeping me out for some reason."

Biz didn't even look at Abler. "Stop always being so scary," he told Pooh. He then continued with Jamal. "We're going to see some girls at the mall. You wanna come?" He asked him.

"I . . . can't," Jamal stuttered. "My dad told me to look after the home until he gets back."

"Why? Ain't nobody gonna steal it."

Pooh started to get impatient. He didn't like Jamal, and saw him as being some kind of threat to his friendship with Biz. This was the new generation of the Tariq, Brooklyn, and Donteer relationship rehashing itself all over again. But this generation was a little more abrasive with no respect for anyone. And for a follower, Pooh was very aggressive. He was ready to leave. "I told you we was wasting our time with this dude," he told Biz.

"No we're not," Biz asserted calmly. "Jamal wants to be down with our clique, he just needs to be asked a certain way."

Pooh laughed, then looked at Jamal with a serious face. "Are we gonna ask him in that way today?" he said, looking into Jamal's eyes.

Clearly, Pooh wanted to get physical, but when Biz looked over Jamal's shoulder at Abler, he appeared thoughtful. "No, we'll do it another time. You should make up your mind, Jamal, what you're gonna do cause this ain't just gonna go away."

Biz and Pooh then walked away, with Pooh still looking back at Jamal. As they got down the block, something strange happened. While they were walking away, and got further down the block, as if by some strange occurrence, even as they spoke in a low tone, Jamal was able to hear their conversation clearly.

"I don't even know why you want him down," Pooh said to Biz. "He's a lame."

"Yeah I know, but there's strength in numbers." Biz looked back, smiled, turned away, and kept walking.

Jamal knew they were trouble makers, but now he knew for sure that they were actually trying to use him. He turned and headed for the porch with his head down, thinking about what had happened. He was also a bit embarrassed, and attempted to walk pass Abler but Abler blocked his path. "You don't have to be afraid of them," he assured Jamal.

"I'm not," Jamal responded, looking down.

"That's good," Abler stated. "But if you were, it would be okay."

Jamal looked at him, thought for a second and smiled. "I think they wanted to try something but were afraid themselves," he told Abler.

"What do you think they were afraid of?" Abler probed.

"You! They thought you had my back."

"I did," Abler responded.

Jamal looked at Abler intently to see if he was serious but Abler started smiling.

"Way back here!" added Abler. They enjoyed a moment of laughter, but Abler then spoke in a very serious tone. "You don't need me to have your back, Jamal. God has your back, and there is no greater security force in existence."

Jamal nodded his head affirmatively, and they both went inside. Jamal went to his room to think some more. Abler wanted to see his grandmother, but Jamal told him that his grandparents weren't up yet, that they usually slept late on Saturdays. So Abler headed back to the guest room.

❋ ❋ ❋

On his way there Abler heard rap music coming from Keesha's room. The music was sort of loud, overshadowing the indistinct sounds of Keesha talking to her friend Kim. Abler knocked, and a few seconds later the music was turned down as Keesha opened the door. Her hair was fully braided and she looked very pretty as she stood there looking at the man who was mugged and beaten up the night before. "Good morning, are you Keesha?" he asked her.

"Yes."

"I'm Abler, thanks for getting the pillow for my head last night."

"You're welcome . . . how'd you know I did that?" she asked curiously.

"I have my sources," Abler said smiling. "Can I come in?"

"Yeah, I guess so," she responded hesitantly.

Keesha stepped aside, leaving the door opened. As Abler entered, she shrugged her shoulders at Kim, who was even more startled. Abler glanced in the mirror over the make-up counter, then he turned to Kim as Keesha walked over. "Hello . . . you are?" he asked her.

"Kim, I'm a friend of Keesha's. You're the man that got beat up and robbed last night?" she asked, bluntly.

It was almost as if Kim couldn't help herself. Keesha checked her immediately. "Kim don't say that!" she stated. "That's not nice."

"What? I just asked a question," Kim said, innocently shrugging. Abler thought it was cute. So young, so innocent, he thought to himself.

"It's all right," Abler responded. "You're blunt. Guess that's close to being honest, right?"

"Right," Kim affirmed, smiling at Keesha.

"Don't encourage her," Keesha told Abler. "She'll hurt your feelings in a heartbeat."

Abler pointed to the chair before the make-up counter. "May I sit for a moment?" he asked.

"If you need to," Keesha consented.

Abler took a seat while the girls sat down on the bed across from him. He looked around the room then his focus landed back on them. "Yes, I was assailed and my charges were taken."

Again Kim exploited the opportunity. "Assailed! It looks like they beat you up," she snapped, looking up at his head.

Keesha rolled her eyes at Kim and shook her head disapprovingly as Abler relented touching his bandaged head.

"I guess you're right," he conceded.

Abler then heard Mildred's voice in the hallway.

He looked towards the room's opened door. While he looked away, Kim stuck her tongue out at Keesha. When Abler looked back again at Keesha and Kim, they both were looking him in the face.

"Please excuse me," he added. "I didn't mean to look away in the middle of our conversation. That was impolite of me."

"That's okay," Kim replied. "People always look away when I am talking to them."

"It happens to me too," Keesha added. "It's not a big deal."

"Oh . . . that's odd," said Abler. "Where I'm from, when a person is conversing with another person, the speaker and the listener always give each other their undivided attention."

"As a matter of respect?" Keesha inquired.

"Certainly," he said. "And because it is a sign."

"A sign of what?" Keesha asked, getting interested.

"Honesty. Many people have hidden agendas. Many people lie, and others simply aren't interested. A tell-tale sign for spotting any of the three, is to watch what a person's eyes do, along with their body language, while you speak with them."

Kim nodded her head, as Keesha thought about what he said. She wanted him to explain further. "What am I looking for in their eyes, and body language?" she asked.

"The eyes of somebody with a hidden agenda will usually divert from your gaze. It's very hard to pull the wool over someone's eye when they're looking in yours."

Kim disagreed. "People do it," she replied.

"Yes they do, but it takes someone far advanced in the use of deception. Many people aren't as skillful at it as they may think."

Keesha was soaking all this up. She wasn't sure if Mark really liked her, and could use these helpful tips to help her find out. "And the body?" she inquired, wanting to know all the details.

"Will usually give them away even further," Abler continued. "Some may sweat, twitch, or fidget. They may cross their arms across their chest. Or tap their fingers or feet. This is done as a defense and distraction."

Just as he said this, Leonard came to the door looking for Abler.

"There you are," Leonard said. "I thought you might have gotten on your way. Can I have a word with you?" he asked.

"Sure," Abler responded, standing up. He then turned back to Keesha and Kim. "Young ladies," he excused himself, "it was nice meeting you both."

Both of the girls smiled and politely nodded as Abler walked toward the doorway, exiting the room. While walking, Abler behind Leonard, Leonard turned back to him. "My wife is down in the living room," he told Abler. "I believe she wants to speak with you as well. Why don't we talk there?"

"Okay," Abler responded politely, as the two men walked pass April and Donteer's bedroom. The door was opened. Leonard kept walking straight ahead as Abler turned and looked into the room, glancing at the chart that said April Shower, and continuing in route to the living room.

CHAPTER 14

Leonard and Abler entered the living room just as Mildred was on her cell-phone expressing her complaint to a supervisor of the Emergency Medical Services. She was clearly disappointed with their service the night before. "Sir, I understand what you're saying," she said into the phone. "There was a great number of calls last night, and your dispatchers were overwhelmed." Leonard took a seat right next to her on the couch, while motioning to Abler to have a seat in the chair across from them. Mildred was still on the phone. "I don't care!" she continued. "I called about a medical emergency that, fortunately, we got through." She looked at Abler for a moment as she said this, then she continued. "Well I'll be filing a complaint. If for no other reason, to make sure that such incidents don't take place in the future. Have a good day sir!" She hung up the phone to her side and, clearly frustrated, turned to Abler. "Excuse me," she said to him. "I was expressing a complaint with the city's Emergency Medical Services. We called an ambulance for you but one never came."

"I don't know what to say," he responded, "except for, thank God I crossed your path. Thank you, I'm very grateful."

"You're welcome," she said as her countenance began to change. How pleasant, she thought, that the first word to come out of his mouth was to thank God. "I'm Mildred. This is my husband, Leonard."

"Nice to meet you both . . . Abler Pen."

"My son told us that you work for a messenger service," Leonard said inquisitively.

Mildred smiled and corrected Leonard. "A Christian messenger service."

Leonard quickly became frustrated. He was trying to find out more about this stranger in their home, and he thought she was being naïve. As the man of the home, he felt he had the responsibility to protect his family, but Donteer, and now his own wife were undermining his authority.

"What's the difference, Mildred?" he asked her, turning to face her.

"There's a big difference," she answered.

Abler, smiling and noticing the tension, cut in. "There is. Our services are very important to the lives of our clients. Somewhat like the Emergency Medical Services, only we actually show up . . . on time." He succeeded in breaking the ice and loosening the tension in the room. Leonard now refocused his attention to him, and Mildred smiled.

"Your vehicle was taken, along with your packages?" she asked him.

"I'm afraid so," he responded. "This troubles me deeply, but I trust that God will make a way. It's all in his hands, even my very life."

Mildred felt a jolt inside as she thought about what he said, but Leonard still wasn't quite convinced. "You'll be all right. I'm sure everything was insured," he said to Abler.

"Some things are beyond indemnification, Mr. Brown. Let's say, for instance, that God had a life changing message or package for you and it was misplaced. How could I compensate you for that?"

"Honestly, I doubt God would send me anything because we haven't been on speaking terms in a while."

The subject of God had always made Leonard act puerile, but it was because he didn't truly believe in God.

"Leonard stop that!" Mildred responded. "The man is just trying to illustrate the value of the articles taken from him."

Even though Mildred was right, Abler used this as an opportunity to encourage Leonard to believe in God. "Perhaps you should think about repairing your relationship with God then. It's always the right time to do the right thing."

Suddenly, Abler began to feel a pain in his head. He touched it, closing his eyes, and Mildred immediately noticed. "Are you all right, Mr. Pen?" she asked.

A second later, he opened back his eyes. "I think I should lie down," he responded.

Mildred, turning to Leonard, joking and hoping to lighten Abler up with a laugh, said, "See Leonard, You've upset the man."

Neither Abler nor Leonard was amused. Leonard, rather skeptical, responded to Abler, saying, "If talking upsets you, sir, maybe you're not all right."

"I'll be all right," Abler assured them both. "I just have to rest for a while."

"You sure?" Leonard asked him.

"Leonard, help the man to the guest room, will you dear?" Mildred urged.

Leonard stood up, but still sort of skeptical. "Okay," he said, "but his life is in God's hands not mine."

Leonard and Abler then left together.

CHAPTER 15

"Oh dear, how is she?" Mildred asked April, as she and Donteer came back from Sheila's. They returned about a half hour after Leonard and Abler went up to the guest room. Mildred stood up briefly hugging April who looked exhausted and a bit shook up as they entered the living room. In fact, she choked up some, but managed to get her words out. "She's still fighting," she responded.

The two women sat down on the couch. Donteer was still standing in the middle of the room, looking at them.

"I know that's right," Mildred said to April, as if she was speaking to her also. She thought April was just going through the motions, that inwardly she had already given up hope. "Sheila was always tough as nails," Mildred added.

"Where's everybody?" Donteer asked his mom.

"The kids are in their rooms. Keesha has company, and Leonard just took Mr. Pen up to the guest room."

Donteer perked up. "He was up and about?" he asked her.

"Briefly," she responded. "When he began speaking about his deliveries, he seemed to be overwhelmed."

Donteer turned to walk over to the doorway when his mother stopped him. "Donteer," she inquired, with her face now turning serious. "The men that robbed Mr. Pen, you know who they are?"

"I have an idea."

"It's no way that we could convince them to return his property?"

"I don't think so mom. It's probably gone by now. And they're not too fond of me."

Mildred sighed as April looked concerned. "What are you asking him mom?" asked April, curiously.

"I don't know," Mildred responded. "I just feel a very strong Christian need to help Mr. Pen recover his property. I think it's important."

"Yeah, but I don't want Donteer getting hurt, or playing police. The last thing we need is for him to go back to prison and leave us out here. We need him."

Donteer understood what his mom was saying. In fact, he felt the same way. But he also understood his wife's position. He just couldn't put his wife through any more stress, especially not after all she's been going through. "I feel something," he said to both of them. "I don't know if it's a sense of duty, or the Spirit, or what. But I can't afford to do anything that can cause me to go back. I have a responsibility to my family first."

Mildred still looked concerned, but April was relieved. He then left and went to the guest room.

❋ ❋ ❋

"If there is a God," Leonard asked, as he leaned on one side of the doorway while Abler laid down, "then why doesn't He just show himself? Because I would love to meet Him."

"He will . . . eventually," Abler responded. "But for now you must believe Him. Look around you. He laid all of the creation before you just for you to acknowledge and believe in Him. Next time you look in the mirror," Abler continued, "ask yourself, Who created me? God doesn't make any mistakes, Mr. Brown. You are at the summit of all His creations, even above His Angels. You're more special than you think. He shed blood for you."

Leonard listened intently as he thought to himself. Could this really be the case, he wondered.

"God loves you so much Mr. Brown, if only you knew."

Mr. Brown then broke his silence. "Why do I need God? I mean, really. I am not some criminal or drug addict. I know what it means to handle responsibility. I've done so for forty years. Never robbed anyone or took anything that wasn't mine. Not that I can remember anyway. I've worked damn hard taking care of my family, protecting and providing for them. Where was God, or some Jesus then. I didn't see him coming trying to help take a load off my hands. And now that I'm old and trying to enjoy the rest of my life He wants to come take credit for what I have done. Does that sound logical, or even fair, to you?"

"That depends."

"On what?"

"On what you consider logical or fair!" Mr. Brown thought for a second, as Abler explained further. "What if I told you that everything you have done so far, though admirable or honorable, was not fair to God?"

"I'd say you're sicker than I thought." Leonard said, laughing.

"Well, think about it. What if, after working so hard to take care of your son, Donteer, he took off and left you without even thanking you or showing any appreciation for everything you've done for him. What if, after giving him life and caring for him . . . after feeding him, protecting him, and raising him up . . . what if after showing him *your* love, he didn't return his love. It's obvious that you love your family." Abler looked around the room then back to Mr. Brown. "But if they all left you in this big ole house and never returned, not even once. They all went on to live their lives. How would *you* feel?"

Leonard thought for a few seconds. "Not good."

"I didn't think so. But that's what you did to God, Mr. Brown. When you was formed in your mother's womb, He had a plan for your life. He took care of you as a child, a teenager, and He's still taking great care of you now. But you turned your back on Him. You lived your life apart from the One who gave it to you, without even stopping by to say thank you. You ran off Mr. Brown. But He didn't forget you. In fact, He wants to give you more life—one that is beyond this world. That's why His Son gave His life, so that you can have it. Now you can have His eternal life in you, along with an eternal relationship with *Our Heavenly Father.*

❋ ❋ ❋

Jamal laid in the bed staring at the ceiling. He'd been going over everything in his mind that took place earlier with Biz and Pooh. Somehow he didn't feel as scared of them as he was before. Was it how confident Abler looked as he stood there on the porch? Was it the fact that his presence kinda scared them off? Or, was it what he said about God watching over him? Jamal contemplated, as he stared up at the ceiling.

Donteer knocked on the door just as he was laying in his bed.

Knock, knock.

"Come in!" Jamal responded.

Donteer stuck his head into Jamal's room. "What's up Peanut?" he asked.

"Just thinking dad!" Jamal was hoping that his father would come in and help him sort the things out that were running through his mind.

Donteer knew something was going on with Jamal. He just didn't have the time. He was only checking in on his way to see Abler.

"Don't think too hard, you may pop that bean head," Donteer replied smiling, and then he left.

* * *

"But why are there so many religions and denominations, all claiming to have the truth? And why are these pastors so corrupt?" Leonard asked Abler.

"It's all about Jesus," he responded. "He is the truth. His words are truth. He is the standard. To the extent of which man deviates from Him and His words is the extent of which many different denominations and religions arise. He never founded a religion, He founded a kingdom—the kingdom of God," Abler stated firmly. "Churches and the pastors that oversee them are just the vehicles used to bring members into God's kingdom. Some vehicles are less effective than others. Some aren't effective at all. But when churches, pastors, members, and you, Mr. Brown, are ready to follow Christ, He will lead you in the way of the kingdom. He wants to lead us; we just have to be willing to follow him . . . all the way."

❋ ❋ ❋

"Come in," Keesha said, after Donteer knocked on the door. He opened it, sticking his head in. "Hey daddy," she greeted him with a smile.

"What's up baby?" He responded to her. Then he greeted Kim, "Hello Kim!"

"Hi Mr. Brown!" she replied smiling.

"Why both of you smiling at me looking all suspicious? What ya'll up to?"

They both busted out laughing as Donteer smiled, backing out the room. He was happy to see Keesha in such a good mood, especially after the previous night.

"So tell me Keesha," Kim begged, as they resumed their conversation. "What did Mark ask you?"

❋ ❋ ❋

Leonard was still standing by the doorway, now just a little more inside the room. Abler was now sitting on the bed facing him. Leonard turned his head just in time to see Donteer, as he approached and entered the room.

"I'll let you take it from here," he told his son. "I can't take too much preaching. He's a walking sermon." Leonard then left.

Donteer knew that Abler can really go when it came to speaking about the Lord. But he also knew that his dad had a very low tolerance for that Christian stuff, as he would put it. Leonard was mainly concerned about Abler's health. His main concern was to get Abler on his way. Donteer looked at Abler, who was now looking himself in the mirror. "What happened?" he inquired of Abler.

"Your father has a good heart. He has a low tolerance for anything spiritual, but it's because it's so much he doesn't understand."

"I can see that. I feel the same way sometimes too."

"I suspect that everyone does. We aren't meant to understand everything of God. However, we must believe Him."

"I guess it always come back to faith."

"Yes. He who created everything, knows everything, and their purpose. All we have to do is trust Him." Abler laid down looking up to the ceiling. "I think I over-exerted myself. Do you mind if I rest?"

"Not at all." Donteer gazed at Abler, who then dozed off.

CHAPTER 16

Jay Z and Alicia Keys', 'New York' blasted through the sound system and the pool tables were all occupied throughout the game room. There was a good amount of people scattered around drinking, smoking, and mingling. Brooklyn and Redd were playing a game of pool on a table off to the side. They were in front of Tariq, who was in his mack-daddy mode speaking to a very pretty woman. He was seated on a stool at the very first pooltable in front of the bar. He held the poolstick in his hands. Its other end was on the floor right between his legs.

When Donteer entered the place, the first thing he noticed was a cloud of smoke over the three rows of pooltables. He greeted a man at another table with a handshake, then saw Tariq and walked over. They exchanged icy looks for a moment, then Donteer broke the ice. "What's up?" he greeted Tariq.

Gamerooms are usually filled with tension. Wherever money is involved, people are usually on edge. And contrary to what most of them thought, the alcohol and weed didn't pacify the situation any. In fact, they fueled the tension level. Donteer knew how tense the game-room can be. He even thought he smelled someone smoking crack as he walked over to where Tariq was. He knew the place was definitely loaded with guns, as mostly everyone there came strapped.

Tariq knew this time would come eventually. The hood is a small world. Even though Donteer was ducking him, he knew they would eventually bump heads somehow, somewhere. He just didn't expect it to be in the game room. "I don't know," was Tariq's response to Donteer's greeting. "You tell me. What brings a freshly minted choir boy like yourself down to the den of thieves?"

"I'm not a choir boy Tariq. I'm just born-again. I don't even go to church like that."

Brooklyn and Redd stopped playing pool and watched the exchange between the two. They too were surprised to see Donteer in the game room. They both were talking to a couple of girls as they played but then now tried to listen to Donteer and Tariq's conversation.

"Yo I really don't care!" Tariq replied cutting to the chase. "What do you want?"

"I want to talk about the incident last night."

"What incident?"

"On the corner."

Tariq couldn't believe his ears. Even though they weren't tight anymore, he thought they had a mutual respect for each other that would prevent Donteer from even approaching him about certain things. This was one. Tariq turned to the woman. "Excuse me for a minute," he said. Then he turned back to Donteer. "What are you, an informant or something? Why you come up in here talking to me about street crime?"

Calling someone a snitch is tantamount to punching them in the face, especially around other people. But Donteer was confident in who he was and didn't particularly feel the need to defend himself. "You know me better than that Tariq. I ain't never tell on nobody."

"I don't know you, my homie's been gone."

"I'm not gonna get into that. I need the stuff that was taken from that messenger outside of Pedro's store." Donteer looked briefly at Brooklyn. "There are some articles in that station wagon that can save someone's life."

"Wasn't no medicine in there," Brooklyn shot back almost immediately but Tariq cut his eyes at Brooklyn, indicating for him to stop talking. And he continued to put Donteer in his place.

"The hell it ain't. You come down here asking me a favor after we haven't spoken in years. Man get out of here!"

Donteer paused, as Redd snickered. Brooklyn then echoed his boy Tariq. "You heard what the man said. Break out cuz!" He placed his hand under his shirt, grabbing the handle of the .38 caliber tucked tightly in his jeans.

Donteer looked at the three of them before he nodded and walked away. Redd set up another game, and Brooklyn just had to get the last word in as Donteer walked out. "That fool thinks because he's born again, he can't die." He said it loud enough for Donteer to hear but he kept walking as though he didn't hear Brooklyn's snide remark. "Yo Ta, what's up with your man, rolling up in here like that?" Brooklyn said, now turning his attention to Tariq. "What he sipping, holy water? He better go ahead. Dudes like that I'll have washing my drawers up north."

Tariq already knew that Brooklyn was jealous of Donteer. He also knew that, given the right situation, Brooklyn wouldn't hesitate to shoot Donteer, if for no other reason, to impress him. Brooklyn was a loyal soldier for the time being, Tariq thought, but he would be a problem real soon if he doesn't have anything to keep him busy. That's just the nature of the game. Some dudes that are loyal today will flip on you tomorrow, or whenever the pressure is on. Tariq been around Donteer long enough to know that he wouldn't flip. Brooklyn and Redd, on the other hand, will flip given the right situation or the right price.

"Yeah, I hear you homie," Tariq responded to Brooklyn, as he was lining up the white ball to break. "I'll take care of D," he added, about to send the white ball assailing. "Right now we gotta get this paper." Snap, crackle, and pop! All the balls went sailing; three in the corner pockets, two in the side. "We got moves to make."

They'd spoken about the trip to Pennyslvania and decided they'll hit the town hard. All together they needed about fifteen gs, five thousand dollars apiece, to get the drugs they needed. Redd briefed them on what they needed to take to start out, and so Tariq decided they'll take a little of everything, some dope, some crack, and some weed. And, of course the guns for the drama. If they played their cards right, that fifteen thousand would kick back sixty.

❋ ❋ ❋

Back home, Donteer and April were laying in the bed. She was dressed in a night gown and the light was on as Donteer entered the room. He could not share the details of what happened at the game room. He knew that would make her even more stressed out and frustrated than she already was so he simply kept it to himself. "Mom said you wanted to turn in early tonight," he said. "You're not having dinner?"

"I'm not hungry, Don."

"You're worried?" he asked, already knowing the answer.

"I can't help it. I'm tired of fighting this illness."

Donteer pointed to her treatment chart. "The worse part is over hon. You documented it," he reaffirmed. "Your oncologist said that we caught it early."

A lone tear rolled down her cheek. "I can't do the radiation again, or the chemo," she said crying. "I just can't."

He hugged and comforted her, as she cried. "You won't have to hon," he continued to console her.

"I'm sorry for not being as strong as you want me to be," she murmured.

"Nonsense, you've been courageous throughout this ordeal. And I know God's grace has been more than sufficient in your life, in our lives."

She backed up to look into his eyes as he spoke to her. He had a way of comforting her that even she couldn't understand. April knew that she had been miserable, but what she couldn't understand was why he didn't just leave her alone and let her fall apart. It was times like those that solidified their bond. Time and again, with every test, her husband rose to the challenge and proved his love to her. "We can't give up on him now," he continued, still looking into her eyes, "because he hasn't given up on us. We may not understand but we have to trust him. His love is more than sufficient." Donteer kissed her on the forehead. "I see him in you baby. I see his strength even in your weakness." This time a tear fell from each of his eyes, one after the other. "God got us," he continued as he squeezed her tight.

Once again April was comforted. She felt renewed and revived. And it was because of him, "Thank you," she said. She really appreciated him. If only he knew.

CHAPTER 17

Inside the conference room of Faith Community Church, Pastor Kelly, his wife Karen, and his treasurer, Levi James, were gathered together with the deacon board to have a leadership meeting. The deacons in attendance were Clarence Tucker, Anthony Carter, Lionel Norton, Marlon Woods, and Sherman Roberts. After a few idle chit-chatter, the meeting was ready to commence.

Karen was trying to take notes and everyone was still talking so she called attention to the meeting. "Excuse me," she interrupted, "I can't take my notes with everyone talking at once."

The last meeting the previous month had ended in a discussion about the financial status of the church so Pastor Kelly, the chairman, convened. "Let's talk one at a time," he asserted. "Anthony, what were you saying?" he asked.

"As I was saying last month," Anthony begun, "we're falling behind in our finances. We may need to add an additional offering to the service."

Lionel supported the motion. "He's right!" he concurred. "The church is about to fall apart into disrepair. And I need some more funds to take care of some things."

Without giving it too much thought, or prayer, Pastor Kelly consented. "So we'll send the plate around one more time for a Pastor's love offering."

Pastor Kelly had started out as a genuine shepherd, caring for the souls of the sheep, but he slowly degenerated into a hireling. He no longer cared about anyone but himself. Besides himself, his main priority had become money, and then, maybe his wife. And this sluggish attitude affected every aspect of his church. In this instance it was seen among the leadership.

Luckily, Pastor Kelly still had a few faithful servants around him, like Sherman. "Pastor Kelly," Sherman objected, "I don't think that collecting more money from our congregation is the answer," he state firmly.

"Well, what do you suggest Sherman?" asked Levi the treasurer.

"Levi, I'm not quite sure but we didn't do it like this in the old days," he answered.

"With all due respect Sherman," Marlon interjected, "this is not yesteryear. You may still wear clothes from the sixties but everyone else has advanced."

For some strange reason, Marlon and Sherman could never seem to see eye to eye during their meetings. Sometimes their disagreements were even bitter.

"Let's keep it respectful gentlemen," Clarence insisted, attempting to keep the meeting focused.

Sherman felt like he was always picked on for being eccentric, as he would put it, as though his ideas were less spiritual. But to him, everyone especially Marlon was carnal and no longer cared about the Father's business. "I'm not trying to rile anyone up," he told him, "especially not you Marlon."

"What's that suppose to mean?" Marlon contended, adding a deadly stare. Noticing that the meeting was beginning to lose direction, the chairman tried to bring some order.

"Let him speak," Pastor Kelly asserted, "and maybe you'll find out. Go ahead Sherman."

"So many members of our church are experiencing difficult financial times," Sherman continued.

Pastor Kelly really didn't appreciate Sherman steering the meeting but tried his best to be patient, that is, until Sherman seemed to be usurping his authority. "I'm experiencing difficult times too Sherman, but that doesn't mean that I'm gonna stop giving to the Lord's house. I give him all my time when I could be doing something else and making more money."

Sherman shot him a deadly stare. "Why, you make enough now," he stated firmly.

Everything froze at this comment. Sherman wasn't quite sure if that slipped out or he actually meant to say it but to him it was the truth. Even Karen stopped taking notes, thinking that Sherman was really overstepping his boundaries. But Pastor Kelly would not have him undermine his authority.

"What did you say?" He asked incredulously. "I lead this church, therefore my salary is appropriate! What are you here for? . . . to assist me! If you didn't know . . . if you can't remember that, maybe you should leave."

"Daniel . . ." His wife attempted to calm him down.

"No Karen, stay out of this. Maybe you'd like to cut some of your salary, Sherman, to help Faith Community make it's way."

"Gladly," Sherman replied. He then looked over to Levi, who was sitting next to Pastor Kelly. "Levi, you're the treasurer. See that it's done."

"Okay Sherman," Levi confirmed.

But then Sherman focused his attention on him.

"I shouldn't even be making this argument, you should as treasurer. You know that the church has fallen behind, yet you say nothing. What type of financial officer are you?" he asked.

"One that trusts his pastor." Levi answered immediately.

"Thank you Levi," the pastor said to his treasurer.

Pastor Kelly didn't for one moment believe Levi. He knew perfectly well that Levi was driven by his own personal motives, as he was, but for the purpose of making him look good in his argument against Sherman, Levi served well.

"What type of deacon are you, Sherman?" Levi retorted.

"One that pays attention to the needs of our flock. For three weeks straight, Sister Parker has put a button in the collection plate. She used to be one of our most generous members."

"What are you getting at?" Levi asked, now getting impatient with Sherman and his bleeding heart.

"The fact that we have members suffering, Levi. They give from credit cards that they can't pay back, and many are out of work. We need to start our free lunch program back, and the Widow Assistance Fund."

"That's enough!" barked the chairman, standing up. "I've heard enough. This isn't our flock. It's mine!" he stated flatly. "We're not restarting any nostalgic programs," he then asserted. "That time has passed. Meeting adjourned."

Everyone else collected their belongings and rose from the table. Sherman remained seated. Anthony and Marlon left the room first. Levi got the pastor's attention and called him over to a corner of the room. He had a ledger in his hand that he attempted to show the Pastor. "What are you doing, Levi? Didn't I say this meeting was over?"

"Yes, but I've been trying to discuss our debts with you for a few months now, and never found the time."

"Levi, I told you to handle it, not bring it up to me at every meeting. You had the chance to say that your job responsibilities were too much when Sherman asked you about them."

"I . . ."

Pastor Kelly cut him off. "No! You didn't say that they were, so find the money."

Karen waited for her husband by the door. He walked over and they left together. Sherman was still seated. He watched the entire conversation between Pastor Kelly and Levi. Sherman and Levi were the last two left in the room. Levi then looked at Sherman, and left quickly.

❋ ❋ ❋

"You Know," Marlon said to Anthony as they walked out of the church to their cars. "I'm really getting sick of Sherman's holier than thou attitude. He was totally out of line."

"He's always out of step. He better be careful or Pastor Kelly will sit him right down and give him some time to think about that rebellious spirit that's always rising up in him whenever we're trying to get things done."

"Ain't that the truth!"

They both walked briskly to their luxury cars as though they had other important things to do.

"See ya tomorrow," Marlon told Anthony, as they simultaneously jumped into their cars and sped off.

❋ ❋ ❋

"Daniel, what just happened back there?" Karen asked Pastor Kelly as he maneuvered his Mercedes Benz on to Fulton Street. He had just hung up the phone. He was on his cell phone the entire time since he left the meeting.

"Honestly, I don't know Karen. Sherman seems to have some other agenda besides serving our leadership. He doesn't seem to want to accept the new direction that we're heading in. Whatever his problem is, we'll have to talk because I won't tolerate insubordination of any kind." He weaved his car around the other vehicles on Flatbush Avenue. "God is moving us in a whole new direction," he continued, "and whoever doesn't want to move with his spirit needs to move out the way." He was on his way to Bay Ridge to get five thousand dollars from the man he was just on the phone with, who made a commitment to start sowing monthly seeds with his ministry.

Karen looked out the window, listening in silence as they made their way up the Ave.

❋ ❋ ❋

Meanwhile Sherman sat still in his car, still outside of the church. He bowed his head and prayed. "Lord Jesus, as always I commit my life to you. I'm a bit confused and discouraged. And Lord I'm tired, but I trust that you have everything under control. This church is Yours. My life is Yours. And this car is Yours. So Lord please bring me home safe." He then carefully pulled his car from the curb.

CHAPTER 18

Back in the Brown residence Abler sat up in his bed reading the Bible. There was an empty plate on the bedside dresser and an empty glass. He then closed his eyes at the end of a particular chapter and verse in the Bible just before Donteer entered the room. Donteer saw Abler praying silently, and stopped in front of the bed waiting. Abler then finished his silent prayer. "Amen," he concluded out loud, opened his eyes and looked up at Donteer.

"Excuse me," said Donteer, "I didn't mean to sneak up on you."

"It's quite all right. I was praying."

"How do you feel?" Donteer asked him.

"Blessed! God's word is so refreshing," Abler stated. "Your mother was kind enough to let me borrow one of her Bibles. She has a nice collection."

"Yes, she does," replied Donteer. "I've been meaning to get me a good one," he added.

"What's stopping you?"

"I've been busy."

"I try to let the Lord's word guide me everywhere I go," said Abler, looking up to the ceiling and clutching the Bible tight to his chest. "I'm never too busy for Him. He deserves His time. That way I know when I really need Him, He'll never be too busy for me."

Donteer nodded affirmatively. "I came to get . . ." He pointed to the plate. "You could've eaten with us at the dinner table."

"Yes, I know. But I needed to speak with God so I thought it would be better if I ate alone."

Donteer appeared thoughtful.

"I'd like to accompany you and your family to church tomorrow."

Donteer offered a half a smile. "How'd you know if I'm attending church tomorrow?" he asked.

"It's the Lord's day, why wouldn't you?"

"Because I'm not really welcomed in my wife and mother's church. That's one reason."

"Whether you are welcomed or not, you should never let anyone, nor the enemy, prevent you from worshipping the Lord. That's our chief purpose—to worship and glorify our God."

"I wasn't talking about the enemy preventing me from attending church. I was referring to . . ."

Abler cut him off. " . . . fellow Christians, some of whom the enemy sways away from the way of Christ. Even you yourself have allowed the enemy to infect and influence your mind. You have your faults, and so do our brothers and sisters, but you have to learn how to look pass them. Just as they are focusing on your faults, you're allowing theirs to hinder you. Look beyond."

The truthfulness of Abler's words were piercing. Donteer couldn't believe that he was that transparent.

He felt uncomfortable and tried to throw Abler off. "I was with you for a moment but you are off base."

"Am I?" Abler asked. "Your experience as a prisoner is just that—an experience. Don't allow it to dictate your spiritual life. Don't think that you're the only victim because you were in prison, or that you're prejudiced against," he continued. "Because you're in danger of prejudging others also."

This was all too painfully truthful for Donteer to accept. He had admitted that he went to prison and had gotten saved. And as a result, he was ostracized. But it was too much for him to admit that inwardly he had become just as judgmental as they were. He shook his head, indicating no.

"Don't close your mind to the truth," Abler asserted. "It's the only thing that will make you free."

Donteer began to stir up in anger, raising his voice and trying to cover up his transparency. "You think you know me?" he barked. "How can your truth free me if you don't know my situation? You don't know what I go through. Trust me, you don't know half my struggles."

Abler looked him straight in the eyes and responded calmly. "You're struggling with your past and your new faith. You're struggling to be a good father, husband, son, and man of God in a world that doesn't accept your past." Abler gestured the quote sign with the finger, while making his next statement. "Even your Christian brothers and sisters do not embrace you. In fact, they shun you, and you've begun to shun them back." Donteer began to smile, looking away and shaking his head, again indicating no. But Abler continued to speak looking directly at him. "What you haven't realized," he continued, "is that you've developed an unhealthy attitude towards those in the church, as if you're without fault." Donteer wiped the smile off of his face. "Donteer, they're sinners just like you. They need the Lord's help and guidance just like all the rest of us. He will clean them, you're just called to love them." Donteer then nodded his head in approval of such statements. "You're a good Christian, Donteer. You do good deeds, like how you helped me. But you need to develop the desire to fellowship with the children of God, however imperfect. This will make you completely Christian."

Donteer thought for a few seconds. And Abler waited for him to respond. Donteer then started to smile. "Well I'm going to church tomorrow because my wife needs me to, so maybe I'll get some fellowship then. And you're welcomed to accompany us."

"Thank you," Abler responded.

Donteer walked over, picked up his plate from the dresser, then turned and headed for the door. He stopped and looked back at Abler, who was still looking at him.

"Good night," he told Abler, as if he was indirectly agreeing to the things Abler said.

"Good night," Abler responded. "But, if I might say one more thing," he then requested. "It's a good first step to attend church because you wish to support your wife. But to truly receive the Godly help and relationship that your heart desires, and to truly know him, you must worship God willingly, and from the heart."

Donteer looked at Abler for a few seconds, appreciating everything he told him, then turned and left.

❋ ❋ ❋

"Make sure you tell Marlon to let the ushers know that we're going to do the Pastor's love offering anyway." It was eleven o clock that same evening and Pastor Kelly was now in his office in front of his computer talking on his phone, "Levi, I want you to exert yourself more. Exercise your authority in Christ, brother. You're my treasurer so take charge." Pastor Kelly continued to type his sermon as he spoke into the phone. "And I want to see you tomorrow after the evening service—just you. God is bringing us to a new place and I want to share it with you first.

"All right," Levi responded in the pastor's ear.

"Good night," said Pastor Kelly and abruptly hung up the phone.

CHAPTER 19

Sunday morning, Faith Community Church was packed as usual. There were about three dozen pews immediately in front full of people. One dozen was in front of the pulpit and two to the sides. The church was very spacious, and elaborately decorated with pictures of Pastor Kelly. It had close to a thousand members total. However only about half of them attended on a regular basis.

The choir sang as ushers stood in the aisles, passing the collection plates up and down the pews. When Sister Abigal Parker, Tariq's grandmother, who was seated in a middle pew, received the collection plate she placed a beautiful golden button in it. And, as the ushers were done, they took the collection plates to a side office.

Two pews in front of Mrs. Parker were Abler and Donteer, who sat next to April. On the other side of April was Keesha, Jamal, and Mildred. Abler had on his original dress shirt.

As the choir sang, Levi, Clarence, Karen, and Sherman, who was dressed in mix-matched attire, took the money out of the collection plates. Sherman had the collection plate with the golden button. He then took it out, smiling to himself.

After the choir was finished singing, they took their seats. Pastor Kelly stepped up front before the pulpit to address the congregation. Everyone gave him their undivided attention.

"I'm never tired of the heavenly sounds of our majestic choir," he stated as he opened up. "Some of my deacons believe that many of you come here to service to hear them instead of me." Some of the congregants laughed as the pastor continued. "I hope this is an acknowledgment of how good a job they're doing and not how bad a job I'm doing." Some of the congregation laughed again, while some gestured no shaking their heads.

Pastor Kelly was very charismatic, and a very persuasive preacher. But, when he stepped behind the pulpit, it was no longer about preaching God's Word. It was the main event, and he was the main character. As he looked down from center stage, his eyes landed on Donteer, and then Abler for a moment, then moved on. "I see there are some new faces here today," he said, referring to both Abler and Donteer. Even though Donteer had been there a couple times before, Pastor Kelly forgot him. Since he wasn't a regular church member the pastor didn't remember his face.

Several church members in the pews around where Donteer was sitting turned and looked his way. Some began whispering to the people seated next to them, who looked at him also. Some looks were hostile, others were curious. Donteer turned and whispered to Abler. "You see the looks folks are giving me?" he asked.

"It's always like this. You'd think I was wearing prison pinstripes."

"Need I remind you that Jesus admonished those that looked down upon their neighbors," Abler whispered back. "If they have a relationship with him, he'll admonish them too."

Pastor Kelly continued. "I would like to see more new faces, along with the old familiar ones. We need more new members here at Faith Community to keep up with the mega churches that are popping up all around us." As Pastor Kelly spoke, there was a new aura eminating from his presence. To the naked eye it went unnoticed but there was a certain haughtiness in the way he spoke and moved, as if he was commanding everyone to look at *him* as oppose to listen to the Word of God.

Sherman noticed and watched him skeptically from the side of the elevated stage. The other deacons, who were also in their positions on the stage off to the side of the pastor, were eagerly listening and looking at him as if they were propping him up.

"I want you to go out and make disciples and members of all," the pastor exhorted the congregation. "Bring em in, in the way of Faith Community, and we'll baptize them in the way of the Father, Son, and the Holy Spirit."

Mildred and a few other members were stimulated, clapping energetically. "Praise the Lord," she shouted above the rest. "You tell em, Pastor!"

Donteer looked at his mother and disappointment crossed his face. Then Abler turned to him. "What's the Pastor's name?" he asked Donteer.

"Daniel Kelly," Donteer whispered once again.

Abler looked at Pastor Kelly mysteriously, then turned and gave Levi the same look. "That's the treasurer, correct?"

"Yup, Levi James."

"I have messages for them," he said, looking up at Pastor Kelly as he delivered his sermon. Donteer looked at Abler confused, then also stared at Pastor Kelly.

❋ ❋ ❋

"Yo Ta you aiight?" Brooklyn asked Tariq as they stood in Brooklyn's building smoking weed. Brooklyn and Redd were talking about the girls they had the previous night at the game room, but Tariq was spaced out. "I hope you ain't still dwelling on that fool D. Just give me the word and I'll pop his head off."

Tariq remained quiet.

"Word," Redd added. "You've been kinda quiet since last night." He figured that it was that they had lost some money gambling. "Don't even sweat that lost homie. Tonight we gonna get our money back."

This time, however, Tariq sure enough wasn't thinking about any money. More silence.

"For sure," Brooklyn continued looking at Tariq, "or we gonna have to catch us another vic. It's nothing. You know how we do." Brooklyn extended his hand to pass Tariq the weed, which he took and smoked.

But the last thing on Tariq's mind doing some stick-up; especially with Brooklyn and Redd. He wasn't gonna tell then that though. Neither was he gonna tell them that he was still thinking about what took place with Donteer. He still couldn't believe that Donteer turned his back on him like that. As much as Tariq was caught up in the streets, he always looked up to Donteer, almost like a big brother, even though he was a few months older than Donteer.

Unlike Brooklyn and Redd, Tariq knew Donteer would be somebody someday. And just seeing him the previous night, once again trying to do the right thing, reminded Tariq of how he was wasting his life away. It disgusted him even more that hanging with Brooklyn and Redd was starting to become redundant, just smoking, drinking, and talking about nothing. He missed the days when Him and Donteer would kick it for hours on the stoop. They would talk about everything, about politics, religion, the game; about their families, their futures, and just life in general.

Donteer was the only person Tariq actually trusted and confided in. He told him about his life growing up with his parents, how he was their only child when they died, and that they died when he was twelve years old. And it was after this that Tariq turned to the streets, not caring about anyone or anything besides money.

Speaking with Donteer always brought a sense of purpose to Tariq's mind. He was reminded that his life wasn't an accident, that he wasn't merely stumbling through this world, that a true hustler was able to make better an already bad situation. Furthermore, all of the topics him and Donteer spoke about were without the influence of any weed or liquor impairing their minds. "Yo I'll catch ya'll later," Tariq told Brooklyn and Redd, passing them back the weed and then leaving.

CHAPTER 20

"Thank you baby, you're an angel," said Mrs. Parker to Abler as him and Donteer walked her up the stairs to her brownstone. Abler helped her up to the stairs.

"You're welcome, Mrs. Parker," he told her. She then took out her keys as she approached the door, opened it, let them in, and they entered her living room.

Over the fireplace was a mantel with several photos. There was a photo of Tariq, Mrs. Parker and her late husband, and Tariq's parents. Abler seized the opportunity to compliment her. "This is a lovely home you have, Mrs. Parker."

"Thank you," she responded with a smile. "I don't entertain often. Just my son and surviving daughters, and their kids. That was a nice service today. Don't you think, Donteer?" she asked, immediately turning her attention to him.

"Yes, it was," he replied.

Mrs. Parker noticed that he hadn't been there in over a month. "I was surprised to see you there," she mentioned. "I haven't seen you in church in a while."

"I've been meaning to get back going," Donteer responded. "I just kinda put it off," he said. He didn't feel like explaining why he stopped going, so he left it at that.

"Yeah, I know what you mean. I do the same thing sometimes. Since my Earnest died, church is the only place I go."

Donteer thought to himself how important fellowship is for Mrs. Parker and he took it for granted. Abler glanced at him as though he read his mind.

Abler then pointed to the photos on the mantel. "May I?" he asked Mrs. Parker.

"Go right ahead," she told him. "That's what it's there for."

He got up and went over to the mantel, looking at the photo of Mrs. Parker and her husband when they were younger. "You two made quite a couple."

"Yes we did. We kept the Lord smiling."

"You still prefer to be called Mrs. Parker, even after all this time? Can I ask you why?"

"Because I never intended to be without my husband, and never wished to marry again. Me and Earnest are one. You can say in the Spirit if you want to, but I make no distinction."

"I understand," Abler responded.

"We were more than a couple; we were a Christian family. Earnest, God, and me. You can never be such a family existing alone."

"How long have you been a member of Faith Community Church?"

"For over forty years," she said. "I've seen it move from shepherd to shepherd, not always for the better, but never staying in the hands of the worst."

"What do you think of the current shepherd?" Abler asked.

"I think that he's a good man that just lost his way a little."

"How so?" Abler continued.

"It happens to a lot of God's people," Mrs. Parker posited. "The earthly pleasures pull at them, and they must fight to place themselves back in the Lord's fold. Prosperity should never come before piety, but often it does."

As Abler began to look at Tariq's photo on the mantel, Donteer explained to Mrs. Parker his reason for bringing Abler to see her. "Mrs. Parker, I introduced you to Mr. Pen at church because he is a messenger for a delivery company. By coincidence, he asked me if I knew an Abigal Parker that lived on our block."

"Oh . . ." she said, somewhat confused.

"He had a message for you but was robbed of his charges while in route to see you."

"Oh dear, I'm sorry," she replied, startled.

As he said this, they heard the front door open and close. Abler was on his way over to deliver his message to Mrs. Parker when Tariq entered the living room. His eyes grew wide and anger crossed his face as he stood there looking at Donteer. He didn't notice Abler, who was stooped down talking to Mrs. Parker. Tariq just couldn't believe Donteer was now in his home, especially after their last episode. "What are you doing in my grandmother's house?" he snapped, losing his mind. At this point he could care less that Donteer was probably the only real friend he had. Everything he was thinking about Donteer just a few minutes ago went out the window.

Donteer stood up quickly, even before Tariq started speaking, but Abler continued talking to Mrs. Parker. He whispered in her ear. She placed her right hand over her chest, both astonished and excited that she was totally oblivious to what was taking place between Donteer and Tariq.

Donteer tried to calm him down. "Hold up," he said to Tariq. "I brought your grandmother home from the church."

When Tariq looked over to his grandmother and saw Abler, the man who was robbed and beaten up two nights before by his homeboys, he almost lost his mind. "Why'd you bring this dude in my house?" asked Tariq, now visibly angry. He approached Donteer, but Donteer backed up closer to Mrs. Parker and Abler. Tariq then ran out of the room and towards the back where his bedroom was.

Donteer knew personally what Tariq was capable of. He had both heard of and witnessed Tariq's wrath in the hood. About a year before Donteer went to prison, while he was shooting hoops in the park alone, Tariq killed a guy name Jay in the park. Jay was a friend of them all, but because Jay didn't pay Tariq his money during a dice game that they were playing, Tariq shot him in the chest. All Donteer heard were the two shots coming from the other side of the park. Startled he just left the park only to find out later that it was Tariq.

Brooklyn and Redd were also there, along with a few other neighborhood ruffians, but no one dared say anything about the incident after that, not even Tariq himself. And after that, Donteer remembered that Tariq seemed to have become a gunner, earning his stripes in the hood by always being ready for gunplay. So if there were two things everyone knew about Tariq were: don't mess with his money; and don't be around him when he pulled out his gun.

"We gotta go!" Donteer told Abler, nervously excited. Abler finished talking to Mrs. Parker, stood up straight, and smiled at her. "Come on! Quickly!" He knew they were asking for trouble if they were still in the house when Tariq came back. They hurried out the house.

Just as they exited, Tariq came out behind them with a gun in his hand in broad daylight this Sunday afternoon. He pointed it at Donteer, yelling and causing them to stop. Passerbys, noticing the scene hurriedly crossed the street. When Donteer and Abler turned around, Tariq's .9mm handgun was pointed at Donteer. "You think I'm playing? What I told you?" Tariq retorted with a spark of anger in his eyes.

"Tariq, calm down man!" said Donteer. "I was just helping your grandmother out. My friend had a delivery for her. It was in the vehicle that was stolen the other day."

"What? I should shoot you for bringing my grandmother into our beef."

Tariq really loved his grandmother. She was all he had after his parents died. And, to make matters worse, he felt as though his supposed friend, Donteer, turned his back on him. That really hurt him. There were so many different emotions stirring up within him, and all he needed was a good excuse to let them out. This was perfect, he thought. Not only did he feel like his grandmother's life was just threatened, but his homeboy was now a traitor, hanging out with a potential enemy. They must think he's stupid, or soft, or something. He tightened his grip around the handle of the gun, clenching his teeth as the spark in his eyes became flames. His trigger finger began to itch, inching around the trigger. Just then, Abler walked in front of Donteer as if to protect him. "Why are you getting in front of him?" Tariq asked him. "What, you think you bulletproof?"

"I don't have a problem with you Tariq," Donteer pleaded, moving back in front of Abler. "Neither does he. We were just concerned about your grandmother," he told him humbly.

As he said this, Tariq's grandmother called him from in the house. She heard the commotion outside and came to the door where she saw him with a gun in his hand. "Tariq," she stated loudly. "Come here now."

In the hood, many people lose their lives at this very point, in a split second. But Tariq heard his grandmother's voice and suddenly had a change of heart. At least for now. "You lucky!" he said to Donteer. Then he looked at Abler. "You better not come by here no more!" Tariq lowered the gun, backed up, and entered his house. And with a sigh of relief, Donteer and Abler hurried down the street.

As they walked away, Donteer made sure he let Abler know that he disapproved of his actions. "Don't ever do that again! His problem is with me. You don't want to get shot over something that has nothing to do with you."

"The enemy has control over him," Abler stated. "Lucky for him, he has a praying grandmother."

"What did you tell her anyway?"

"I delivered her message. You were mistaken, her's wasn't tangible it was verbal."

❋ ❋ ❋

"Tell him I'm not here," Pastor Kelly told his wife, speaking of a couple from his congregation, Trevor and Sharon Bailey, who were having problems in their marriage. They were to meet with him the week before but he cancelled on them to attend a seminar the same day on Biblical principles of finance. This time Pastor Kelly was having a meeting with Levi in his office.

"When do you want me to reschedule them for," Karen asked her husband.

"Just tell Mr. Bailey that I'll call him later on tonight," he told her as she left the office.

Karen really didn't approve of her husband lying or encouraging her to do so but she didn't want to bring it up in front of Levi. Usually she'll wait until they're in the confines of their own home, in which he'll blow up, making her feel like she's not supportive towards him. Then she'll feel bad and leave whatever it is at God's throne in prayer.

"So how much did we collect from my love fund?" the Pastor asked Levi, resuming their conversation after Karen left.

"Seven fifty," Levi said nonchalantly, throwing a roll of cash on his table.

"What about tithes?"

"Eleven seventy two," Levi added. "Seems like the wells are dried up. This is the first time I've seen our members so tight."

"Times are different than when we first came on board," Pastor Kelly explained. "We gotta change with the times. What's Lionel teaching on in Bible study this month?"

"I'm not sure," Levi responded. "I think somewhere in the Old Testament."

"Let him know that for the next two months we wanna push the Biblical principles of finance. That's what I wanted to talk to you about. I have some information I picked up from the seminar. While he does that, I'll hammer home the importance of tithing from the pulpit. When the wells get dry, we have to dig," he continued. "There's no way the Lord's house should be in need. How much money do you need?" Pastor Kelly asked Levi, taking the cash from the table.

"I need five hundred. My car note is about due, and I have a date tonight," Levi replied. "You're right, there's no reason why the Lord's house should be in need. Not the way you preach anyway," he added, smiling.

"Just remember, this is off the record."

* * *

Tariq laid in his bed. His head was spinning even faster than the ceiling fan that he was gazing at. He really didn't know what to think. Was he losing his mind, he asked himself. Why was Donteer and this dude in his house? Was Donteer, his homeboy, in his house telling his grandmother about what took place? Do he really have to get Brooklyn or Redd to take care of Donteer? Just when he thought his mind was going to spin out of control, his grandmother knocked on his bedroom door. "Come in grandma, it's open!"

CHAPTER 21

"Mom, can we be excused?" Keesha requested of her mother.

The entire family were eating dinner later on that Sunday evening after the incident with Tariq. Everyone except for Abler were nearly finished eating when Keesha looked at her brother and asked her mom to be excused.

"You can," April told her, then she looked at Jamal. "If you're done, you can be excused also." She smiled as Keesha and Jamal got up. "Leave your plates, I'll get them," she told them.

As they left, Mildred turned and smiled at April. "I think Mr. Pen likes our cooking," she told April as the kids were leaving. Abler responded with a thumbs up because his mouth was stuffed. "Would you like some more?" Mildred then asked.

He nodded affirmatively.

Mildred got up and put some more food on Abler's plate. Everyone else was done eating so she began clearing the table. April stood up and helped her while the men sat and conversed.

"I feel sorry for Mrs. Parker," said Leonard. "With all that woman has been through, she has a criminal for a grandson."

Donteer understood the streets, and the daily pressures of being a young black man in the hood. He understood that from a young age, Tariq was caught up in the game, and that he really didn't know anything else but streetlife and crime. "Dad, Tariq's not really a bad guy," he insisted.

"What," his father responded incredulously, "are you blind too? You already proved you're deaf and dumb. The man is a time bomb. He told you to stay away from him. Why can't you do it?"

Leonard was already frustrated from the whole situation. Even though he had gotten to know that Abler wasn't a bad guy, he was beginning to feel too responsible for him. And it was starting to show. His wife tried to calm him down. "Leonard, we have a guest."

"He was there," Leonard continued, "so I don't have to watch my tongue. He's foolhardy too, if you ask me, stepping in front of a man with a gun."

Abler finished eating, and handed April his plate. "Thank you, I don't eat like this very often," he told her with a smile. He then responded to Leonard's statement. "I don't think what I did was venturesome at all, especially after all that Donteer had done for me."

"Well you better learn the difference between urbane and urban, Mr. Pen," Leonard warned. "Your life may depend on it."

"I really wish people wouldn't worry about this life so much," Abler stated generally to everyone. "Considering the next life is so much more fulfilling."

Everyone stared at Abler when he said this; especially April, who looked like she had a revelation. Mildred, however, really didn't appreciate Leonard's hostility, especially after all the man has been through. He was purposely being belligerent. "Okay, thank you, Leonard, for following up a delightful meal with a degenerated topic," she said. "And, Mr. Pen, you don't have to explain yourself. When the Spirit leads, you just be sure to follow. The best example we have of what you did is the Lord himself. He laid down his life for his friends."

"Thank you, Mrs. Brown," Abler responded immediately, swallowing his food, clearing his throat and looking at her. "But I'm not worthy of being mentioned in the same breath with the Lord Jesus and His sacrifice. Can't no one make a sacrifice such as his."

Leonard didn't know how to argue with this so he simply raised his eyebrow and looked at Abler questionably.

❋ ❋ ❋

"Why do you want to discuss sexually transmitted diseases with me," Jamal asked Keesha, as they stood in her room. "I'm not having sex." Keesha pouted, then Jamal looked curious. "Are you?" he asked her.

"No, not yet," she responded. "But I was thinking about it."

"Keesha, you should be talking to mom or dad, not me."

"I can't talk to them about this, Jamal."

Jamal sighed. "Listen you're too young to be thinking about sex. Boys my age, that's all they think about. So if a boy is pressuring you, sex is all he wants from you, nothing else."

"You can't know that for sure."

"Keesha, I may not know everything, or even a lot, but that I know for sure. Remember when mom explained to us that our bodies are sacred?".

Keesha nodded.

"You believe her?"

"Yeah, but . . ."

"But nothing, Keesha," Jamal asserted. "We have to treat our bodies as such, which means we don't give them away. We honor them."

"Jamal, you're a guy and you're popular. It's different for you."

"Not really! I'm struggling also. Everyone at our ages go through similar struggles. I may have different troubles than you but trust me I'm in a difficult place too."

"So, what do we do?" she asked him.

"We trust mom and dad. And we trust everything that they have taught us so far. I'm not saying that any of our friends would lie to us, but don't believe that they won't." Keesha was comforted, at least for the moment.

"Keep this between me and you, okay?"

"Only if you promise me that you won't let anyone pressure you into doing anything you know isn't right," he told her.

"I promise."

"Okay," Jamal said, as he hugged his sister and then left.

❋ ❋ ❋

"Just the person I was looking for," Donteer told Jamal throwing his arm around his shoulder as he walked into the hallway. They left together and went to Jamal's room. Donteer leaned against the wall by Jamal's room door, as Jamal began to put together his clothes for the next day.

"What's up dad?" he inquired.

"I wanted to tell you that I love you son."

Jamal stopped going through his clothes and looked at his father. "I love you too dad," he reassured Donteer, "but what's up? You're not dying right?"

Donteer laughed. "No, I'm not," he answered.

Jamal still looked alarmed. "Mom?"

"No, no," Donteer responded, still laughing. "I just wanted you to know that. I don't think men tell their sons they love them enough. It's easier to tell a daughter."

"I see. I overheard you telling mom and grandma about what happened earlier at the Parkers. That's what this is all about?"

"Yes, and no. I'd be telling you this even if that didn't happen, if I wasn't so busy. But what took place did make me think of you."

"Why?" Jamal asked, now very curious.

"Because Tariq's mother and father died in a car accident when we were both teenagers. Not saying if they would've lived, he would've turned out much different. But they were both drug addicts, and high most of the time. It was almost as if they didn't know they had a son. I'll never forget how much Mrs. Parker aged when she lost her daughter, Patricia, which was Tariq's mother."

Donteer knew more than anyone, the effect that the lack of parental love had on Tariq. It was even worse that he had no brothers or sisters. When Tariq was four years old, his mom had a miscarriage. A year later she had another one. As far back as Tariq could remember, it was these two events that altered the course of his mother's life. It was these two events that sent her running after that bottle of gin, and his father went after her, and the bottle.

From this point their lives just seemed to spiral downward as they continued down that path, neglecting Lil Tariq, both of their families, their jobs, and everything else besides that bottle of liquor and that stem of crack rock. From a young tender age Tariq saw the slow disintegration of his helpless parents. He actually felt sorry for them, unable to do anything to rescue them from themselves. Besides, he was too young to understand fully the many issues that plagued his parents' lives and other grownups in their shoes. Grandma Parker understood fully what they were going through, but she too was unable to rescue them. She did, however, began to commit all of their lives, including Tariq's, into the hands of the Lord.

Donteer also knew firsthand the effects that can befall someone as neglected as Tariq. And so he felt the need to let his son know that he was loved.

"Dad, I'm on point. I know that you and mom are here if I need you."

"Do you?"

* * *

"Hello, Mark?" Keesha said into the phone.

After Jamal left, she just couldn't resist the urge to call. Like most young girls her age, she thought with her heart and not her mind. All she thought about was being loved and accepted by Mark, and the consequences faded to the background.

"Who's this? Lisa?" he answered, joking.

Keesha didn't know if he was playing or not, but even if he was playing with her there was nothing funny about him calling her another girl's name. "It's Keesha," she said loud enough for him not to confuse it next time.

"I knew that," he responded. Mark knew this would hit a nerve, but it was all part of his plan to make her feel even more insecure and self-conscious. "I'm just playing with you," he said. "What's the deal? Did you think about what I asked you?"

Keesha hesitated for a moment. "Yeah, I thought that you were gonna call me," she replied.

"I was just about to," he said nonchalantly, "but you dialed faster than me."

Keesha laughed.

"So, are we gonna hook up tomorrow, or what?" he asked her straight up.

"I don't know Mark. I don't think I'm ready to have sex," she answered. "What if I get pregnant, or catch a disease?"

"Are you saying I have a disease?"

"No, but . . ."

"Keesha, I'm healthy. And I won't get you pregnant. We can use protection. I love you Keesha, don't you love me?"

Keesha hesitated. "I like you a lot," she said slowly, "but I don't know if that's love."

"It's the same thing."

"Why do you like me, Mark? Because not everyone else does."

"I'm not everyone, Keesha. I'm just me. And I think you're special."

Keesha smiled broadly.

❋ ❋ ❋

Back in the Brown's living room, Mildred, Leonard, and Abler sat watching television. Abler was ready to turn in for the night. He said good night to Mildred and Leonard, then he left. While in the hallway, walking pass April's bedroom, he noticed her on her knees praying with her head on the bed. She was crying out to the Lord loud enough for him to hear her. She felt like someone was looking at her, but by the time she raised her head, Abler was gone.

CHAPTER 22

"I gotta do it like this, dad," Jamal said to Donteer, while sitting on the edge of his bed. Donteer was now seated on a chair, with the high end in front of him.

"Okay, I understand," Donteer replied. "But I want to be in the vicinity."

Jamal had finally mustered up enough courage to face Biz and Pooh. Donteer really didn't want to get involved but he had to make sure his son was confident. Inwardly, however, he couldn't help but to feel a sense of fulfillment knowing his son was becoming a man—standing up—and becoming a leader.

"Peanut, things are much different than when I was your age," Donteer cautioned his son. "As kids we fought but didn't kill one another."

"I know dad." Jamal was still somewhat worried but he knew deep down inside that he had to face Biz and Pooh. And he had to do it alone.

"We gotta start hanging out again," Donteer changed the topic, "going back to ball games and concerts as soon as I get me a job."

"I miss hanging out with you dad."

"I know son. Do you remember why I use to tell you that it was important for you to experience different things, and see different places?" Donteer asked him.

"Sure dad," he answered. "So I could see that I have choices. You said, if you see different people, you'll know that you can be different."

Donteer smiled and extended his fist to his son. He really made him feel proud to be a dad. To know that his teenage son was willing to go against peer pressure and the daily pressures of society to be obedient to his father really made his day. That night Donteer truly saw himself in his son's face. And he liked what he saw.

❋ ❋ ❋

Immediately after talking with Jamal, Donteer went to the laundry room to speak to the Lord. So much had taken place in such a short period of time. He felt as though everyone needed him. His wife needed his strength. His kids needed his guidance. His parents needed his love. And he needed Jesus . . . to be all these things.

Actually he hadn't prayed or read a Bible in a few weeks. When he was in prison he would get up consistently every morning to spend time with the Lord. But since he came home and was preoccupied with getting a job and taking care of his family, he neglected to spend any quality time praying or reading the Bible. Seeing Abler in the bed praying after all he'd been through reminded him of his urgent need to keep God first . . . in all things.

"Lord Jesus," he began broken and humbly. "I need you . . . we need you. I'm tired and weak, and I can't go on without you. April needs your strength to touch her body. Heal her completely, please," he pleaded. "Jamal and Keesha need your guidance, O Lord, lead and protect them. And I need you more than ever. You have always provided for me. Please provide a job so I can help provide for my family, so that I can provide a future for my kids. Help us please, Father. Make a way. And help my faith to grow in you. I wanna be more faithful," he pressed. "Strengthen my faith and help me to be the man you want me to be. And Father, help my boy Tariq. He's been through a lot. But I know you already know that. He's caught up now, but touch his troubled heart that he may know that you love him . . . that you've given him life. And, in spite of all that he's been through, you've created him with a purpose."

❋ ❋ ❋

As Jamal laid in his bed, thoughts running rampant through his mind, he also suddenly felt the urge to pray. He sat up in his bed. And he got on his knees.

His parents and grandmother always encouraged him to pray before he went to sleep but this time the need for God was pressing. He remembered what Abler said about God being his security, and so he sought the Lord's help.

"God . . . I ask that you watch over me," he prayed. "Protect me tomorrow, or whenever I see Biz and Pooh. I don't want no problems with them God but I don't want to be their friend. Sorry for not praying to you every night like I should and I promise I will from now on."

He then laid back down feeling an overwhelming peace and fell fast asleep.

❋ ❋ ❋

"And Father, I wanna serve you," Donteer continued. "Take my life. It's yours. Do with it as you please. Whatever gifts and talents you gave me, is yours. Use them for your glory, Father. I just wanna bring honor to your name."

❋ ❋ ❋

Keesha was still up after she got off the phone with Mark. Her mind also was restless, thinking about what Jamal had told her and her conversation with Mark. What Jamal said made sense to her but she really liked Mark, especially after he told her she was special. However, Keesha was confused. Something wasn't right about the way Mark was pressuring her, she thought. Her parents always told her that she was smart and responsible, and she began to think that she needed to really consider this decision she was about to make, for it would affect her for the rest of her life.

❋ ❋ ❋

April was now laying in their bed reading the gospel of Matthew, and landed where Jesus went about healing all manner of sicknesses and performed many miracles, when Donteer came in the room. He kissed her lightly on her lips and he went to sleep. April stayed up reading a little while longer then she fell asleep also.

But before she could slip into oblivion, she noticed a figure standing before her whom she thought was Jesus. He was extremely luminous so it was unable to tell who he was. Being that she was just reading about Jesus, He was the first person that came to her mind. But when she heard the voice, it sounded like Abler.

"Do you believe," the voice asked, "that Jesus can make you whole?"

As she looked at the figure, trying to make out who it was that spoke to her, she attempted to walk a little closer to him but she felt as though she couldn't walk.

"Do you believe?" she was asked a second time, "that Jesus can make you whole?"

She tried to reach out her hands and touch him but felt as though her arms were bound to her chest.

"Do you believe?" the voice persisted authoritatively, commanding her full attention, "that Jesus can make you whole?"

Feeling totally bound, she tried to cry out but her tongue was held to the roof of her mouth. However, as April stood looking upon this figure, she felt hopeful. This was more than a dream to her. It was as if God was speaking directly to her and her condition through this person—whoever or whatever he was. She didn't know what it was that prevented her from reaching out or responding back . . . but she was determined to change it.

"Yes," she responded but only from within her heart. Her tongue still could not move. But feeling unperturbed, April simply responded from within her heart. "Yes, I believe."

Almost as if the person heard the cry of her heart, he asked her again immediately, "Do . . . you . . . believe?" This time the question was slow, as if April was given time to consider her answer, and respond authoritatively.

Then, feeling more confident, she cried out loudly from the depths of her soul, "Yes," as her entire body shook. "Jesus," she continued with another loud shout from the depths of her heart. This time her words made their way from her heart, through her mouth loosing her tongue completely. "Jesus, I believe that you can make me whole."

When April said His name, the very foundation of the place where they stood shook, and simultaneously, even as she said the name of Jesus, she bolted up in her bed, sweating profusely and her hands extending forward as she was attempting to grab the air over her bed. She then looked over at Donteer, who was still fast asleep. Still breathing hard, she plopped her head back down, staring at the ceiling. "Thank you Lord," she whispered and she fell fast asleep.

CHAPTER 23

The next morning was Monday. Donteer was woken up by a car horn that honked impatiently every few seconds. He woke up and looked out the window, and saw Tariq standing at the curb leaning against Abler's station wagon. His and Donteer's eyes met.

Donteer jumped into his sneakers and hurried downstairs with a tank top tee shirt and a pair of sweatpants on. When he walked outside and approached Tariq at the curb, he met a totally different person than the previous day. Tariq was smiling. "After the other day, I thought you'd come out bearing arms, just not like this," he punned, referring to Donteer's skinny arms that hung out of his tank top.

However, Donteer never cracked a smile. He really didn't appreciate Tariq pulling out a gun on him, but he would have to leave that conversation for another day, he thought. What he did appreciate was that Tariq brought back the station wagon, so he approached Tariq, not giving away his thoughts, but looking in the direction of the station wagon which had packages in the seat.

"What's happening?" he said, looking at the station wagon then at Tariq.

"You were right," Tariq responded. "Our beef ain't got nothing to do with anybody else."

"I don't have any beef," Donteer assured him.

"I did," Tariq countered. "You were my only real friend, D. You knew everything. Then you go to prison for three years, and everything changed."

"It changed for the better, Tariq."

"I know. That's what really hurt," he confessed. "I didn't know, and still don't know how to get to that place."

"You have to expect the best from yourself, Tariq. A life of crime isn't your best. We weren't created to be criminals."

"I'm not out here doing crime; Brooklyn and Redd are. I'm just eating off of them," Tariq said smiling. "I got kids to feed." Donteer started to argue but Tariq stopped him, knowing what Donteer was saying was true. He threw the keys to the station wagon at him. "But I understand," he conceded. "I got back what was left. Some stuff they got rid of. It is what it is." He shrugged his shoulders.

As he was speaking, Donteer sensed something different about Tariq. "Can I help you?" he asked him.

"I don't think so," Tariq answered. "I have to find out on my own like you did. I'm not going to church though."

"Why not?"

"Because I don't like its structure. Those in control manipulate and take advantage of people like my grandmother. But the truly needy don't get anything but a promise of salvation later. It's just another hustle."

"It's more to it than that Tariq. I use to think the same thing, but I realize that it's bigger than them. We all sinners, Ta!"

"Nah D, they worse than me," Tariq maintained. "Because they lining their pockets slinging the Bible. I aint never think of doing nothing like that. They bleeding the community when they supposed to be feeding it homie."

Just as Tariq said this, Abler stepped out on the porch. Both Donteer and Tariq looked at him, briefly, before Donteer resumed the conversation. "We can keep pointing the finger, or we can step our game up and do what we know is right," he added. "What's it gonna be?"

Donteer knew that Tariq was right. There was no way he would even attempt to argue with what he said. In fact he felt the same way but he couldn't allow Tariq to take the easy way out, when he knew good and well that Tariq was responsible for half the drugs that came through their corner of the hood.

"I feel you D, but for now we'll just agree to disagree." Tariq then pointed to Abler. "Homeboy told my grandmother something that made her very happy. She ain't been like that in a very long time. We spoke all night. We kicked it like never before. That's why I'm here now."

Donteer smiled. "That's good, I'm glad," he responded, without looking back at Abler.

"She asked me to change and to be willing to suffer for what is right." Tariq continued. "I'm not there yet, but for her I'll try."

Donteer was very happy to hear this, more happy than he revealed. "That's all any of us can do," he replied.

He knew that Tariq had so much potential in Him but it was only God that could've actually changed his heart. And by the look of things, He had already begun to.

"My grandmother said that she will not be here much longer, and that she's ready to go because your friend told her my grandfather was waiting for her in heaven." Tariq looked both sad and confused when he said this. "I can't even get into that, but thanks. And sorry for everything. You know, my bad with the gun and all. I don't know what got into me." He extended his hand to Donteer.

"It's all good," Donteer reassured Tariq, giving him a pound and a hug. "Make her proud before she leaves," he told him.

Tariq walked away, looking over at Abler then holding his head down. Abler then went over to his station wagon.

"He brought your car back, and most of your parcels." Donteer was excited and relieved. Ever since the moment Abler told him about his lost, he felt responsible in a weird kinda way. Abler extended his hand to get his keys.

"We should hurry!"

Donteer thought for a second, then said, "Hold up, let me change my clothes." And ran up the stairs into his house.

CHAPTER 24

"Why'd you want me to accompany you? You seem to know these streets?" asked Donteer, in the passenger seat. Abler really appreciated Donteer getting his property back and asked him to hang out with him for the day as he made his deliveries. Donteer had on a dress shirt and slacks as if he was working with Abler.

"You never know," he told Donteer, "maybe I can put in a good word for you with my boss."

"You'd do that? I'd definitely appreciate it." Donteer thought for a moment. "You know Tariq said some things about our church that I found hard to defend."

"Did he sound familiar?" Abler asked him smiling.

Donteer smiled. "Yeah, like me making excuses. But some of the things he said were true," he added.

"His grandmother's correct. Pastor Kelly has lost his way. This path is very narrow, Donteer. The closer you get to the end, the more temptations come and the easier it is to slip and fall."

"You're confusing me," Donteer interjected. "You said something to the effect the other day of folks holding their noses high up in the air, acting all self-righteous, not being closer to the kingdom."

"Sometimes that is the case. But God is also merciful," Abler reminded him. "Did you ever think that maybe God allowed him to lose his way in order to make him stronger and wiser?"

"He would do that?"

"God's ways are beyond ours," Abler continued. "His ways are far more perfect, effective, and everlasting. Make no mistake about it, Donteer, the church *is* the Lord's. He is in full control. When bad situations happen in His childrens' lives, it is because *He* allows them to, so that we will turn to Him and be better people in the end."

"Like prison?" asked Donteer, smiling.

Abler smiled. "Like prison," he reaffirmed, as though he was waiting for Donteer to say that.

Abler then pulled over in front of an old dilapidated house. Donteer looked at it surprised.

"You're going in there?" he asked Abler. "I know the woman that lives there, Trisha Truepenny. She was one of Keesha's teachers."

"Then you know how her husband left her after she got pregnant, and how the baby died an infant."

"Yeah, it was sad. She always wanted to be a mother. She loved kids. But she was never the same, I don't even see her anymore."

"She doesn't leave the house," Abler responded, as though he knew her personally.

He started to get out, touching the door knob, but he stopped and turned to Donteer. "You should wait here," he told him.

"Okay, but there's something else I wanted to ask you."

"Which is?"

"What you told Mrs. Parker, you did that just to make her feel good?"

"Why, do you think it worked?"

"Tariq seems to think so. He says she ain't been the same since. That's why he returned your car and packages."

"Then what I told her served its purpose," he said smiling. Abler then exited his car and walked up to Trisha's home, while Donteer watched from the car. Abler was about to knock, when the front door opened. Then Trisha, looking bedraggled, came out and greeted Abler looking at him astonished.

* * *

From the station wagon, Donteer watched Abler as he touched her shoulder and spoke to her briefly. Surprisingly, a moment later, she got happy just as when he spoke to Mrs. Parker. Donteer studied Trisha's smiling face as Abler got back in the station wagon and then he stared at him, confused.

As they drove off, Donteer watched Trisha who was staring behind the car. "I suppose her message wasn't tangible either," he said to Abler.

"That depends on your definition of tangible. I told her that her baby was in heaven. I think that touched her. What you think?"

* * *

"Pastor Kelly, it was unbelieveable," said Levi, speaking to the pastor in his office. "The woman thought I was Levi Stubbs from The Four Tops."

They both laughed.

"She asked me to sing Sugar Pie Honey Bunch," he continued, "and said that it was her favorite song."

"I hope you told her that you don't sing about pies and honey by the bunch, you eat them," the Pastor responded.

They laughed again, as a knock was heard at the door.

"Come in," said Pastor Kelly.

Karen walked in ushering in Abler.

"This man states that he has a message for both of you," she told them.

Pastor Kelly and Levi looked confused, as Abler took out a notice from his pocket and handed it to Pastor Kelly. He read the notice to Levi, who listened intently.

"The bank is foreclosing on the church!" he read, shocked and confused. "This is the final notice," he continued, now startled. "We have thirty days to vacate," Pastor Kelly concluded, raising his head to look at Levi, then at Abler.

"What?" Levi responded, clearly astonished.

Pastor Kelly couldn't believe it. He remembered Abler's face from church the day before. But what he could not understand was why he was in his office, serving a foreclosure notice to both him and Levi.

"What is this, some kind of joke?" asked Pastor Kelly.

"It's no joke. You have failed to honor your pledge, not only to your creditors, but to God. Good day!"

Abler turned and left, leaving Pastor Kelly, Levi, and Karen staring at one another, stunned.

CHAPTER 25

"This is my room," Mark said to Keesha as they walked into his room. "I basically decorated it myself," he said, closing the door behind him.

"Look like it," she said looking around nervously. "Your mother . . ."

" . . . won't be home until late," he cut her off. "I'm suppose to wait for her at my cousin's house. So it's just us."

Keesha nodded, still looking nervous.

"You want me to put on some music?" he asked her, smiling and walking toward his sound system.

"No," she answered, mustering up enough strength to stay in control. "I want to talk."

"Talk," he retorted incredulously. He then approached her and touched her shoulder and cheek. "We can talk later."

"Wait," Keesha demanded. Mark then dropped his hand, sighing. "Are we gonna be together forever?" she asked him.

Mark looked away. "I guess so," he responded.

"And, you love me?"

Again he looked away after looking at her briefly. "I already told you that!" he said, now visibly agitated.

"So tell me again."

This time Mark looked at the wall behind Keesha, trying to mask the way he truly felt. "Yeah, I love you," he said. Then he looked at her.

"Why you keep looking away?"

"What?" Mark responded in a high pitch, sounding even more guilty. He didn't know what to say. He certainly hadn't expected Keesha to be interrogating him.

"Why can't you look at me in my eyes?"

"I . . . I" he stuttered. "I'm looking . . . you."

"You stutter now?" Keesha pushed Mark away from her.

"When I'm nervous," he responded, now attempting to sound sincere but it was a minute too late.

"No, not when you're nervous," she shot back. "When you're lying!"

Keesha backed away from him towards the door.

"Keesha," Mark begged, trying again to sound sincere.

But all of a sudden, everything appeared painfully clear. He was lying the entire time. And he just wanted to use her for sex. Obviously, she wasn't as naïve as he thought. "Get away from me!" she snapped. "You're a liar!" She then walked away from Mark and left his house immediately, hurrying down the block and around the corner to her home.

❋ ❋ ❋

"Yo come out," said Mark as he sat on his bed sulking. "I said come out," he said even louder. He then got up and went over to his closet door, yanking it wide open.

Biz and Pooh were laid out laughing hysterically on his closet floor with their hands on their stomachs.

"I love you," Pooh blurted out as his eyes were tearing from laughter.

"Keesha," Biz followed, mimicking the way Mark sung her voice.

"Get up," Mark said, now furious. "Ya'll gotta go!"

They got up slowly, but still snickering at Mark who walked back over to his bed.

"It ain't our fault you ain't got no game, playboy," Biz said as he led the way out of Mark's house.

CHAPTER 26

The sun was beginning to set. It was seen from Shalom Stein's living room window in Stuyvesant Heights where he sat reading his Bible. There were track and field trophies covering a mantel in the room. And a portrait of Shalom running and winning a major race was over the fireplace.

As he was reading, the door bell rang. He put the Bible down and got up. At the door was Abler and Donteer. Abler had a box in his hand.

"Yes, may I help?" Mr. Stein asked them both.

"Mr. Shalom Stein?" Abler asked.

"Yes," he answered, now wearing a curious look on his face.

"Are you still running?" Abler continued.

"Oh no," he replied, smiling. "In my younger days. I haven't ran in quite a long time. I revel at the idea of a challenge to a race but, I'm sorry, those days are over."

"We're not here to challenge you sir," Abler said. "Just came to return something you lost."

Abler handed the pastor the parcel. Mr. Stein opened it, and immediately fell to his knees, after which he began to cry.

"Thank you!" he muttered. "Thank you! Where . . ."

Abler and Donteer helped him up to his feet. As they did, Mr. Stein explained.

"Wow, this was my very last trophy from the last race I ran over twenty five years ago. I lost it when I was moving here," he said, looking at the trophy. "I dedicated this trophy to the Lord, and made a vow that from that day till the day I die . . ." He began to cry. "I . . . will serve him. I will run the race of life serving Christ."

Abler was smiling but Donteer was very confused. He tried to cheer Mr. Stein up. "You're making me sad, sir. You should be happy." Donteer said as he smiled reassuringly. "You found something priceless that was lost."

Mr. Stein was still crying, but he muttered back to Donteer. "You don't understand. I haven't kept my vow to serve the Lord till I die. You see, I'm a pastor, but I haven't been a faithful one. My wife left me three years ago, and ever since then my heart has gotten cold. I retired and deserted the Lord's sheep."

Abler nodded his head to everything Mr. Stein said, but in a rather consoling way. Then he responded back to him. "Well it looks like the Lord has forgiven you," he said to Mr. Stein. "Don't beat yourself up any longer. We all fall down some time or another. Just pick yourself up, dust yourself off, and keep on running. The Lord hasn't left you. He's waiting for you at the finish line with your eternal reward. Return to your first love, Pastor Stein. Keep going!"

Abler and Donteer turned and left, as Donteer said goodbye. "Have a good day!"

Mr. Stein just nodded his head in a slow confused way and stared after them.

❋ ❋ ❋

"Honey!" Donteer yelled, walking into the house with Abler after a long and exciting day.

They entered the living room and Donteer was about to yell again when they saw April, Mildred, Leonard, Keesha and Jamal sitting there. The mood suddenly became very somber. April and Mildred were crying.

"What is it?" Donteer asked them.

April got up, went to Donteer and hugged him. "Sheila died this morning," she said, with tears running down her cheek.

Donteer was stuck in shock for a few seconds. He was just on a high from such a mind boggling day, and then this—his friend for so many years, gone. Sheila was such a good source of encouragement and strength for him and April, both before and during her illness. He would never forget her, he thought, especially their last visit at her house when she was stronger than ever, almost as if she knew she was going to die. "May God bless her soul," he prayed secretly, looking up with tears in his eyes, as April rested her head on his chest.

❋ ❋ ❋

"Celo!" yelled Brooklyn, then collected money from the other three guys playing dice, including Redd. They were in the park for the past few hours that day playing, and Brooklyn finally won back the money he had lost, breaking even. "Yo we out!" he said to the other two guys as him and Redd headed out of the park. Brooklyn then turned to Redd as they left. "What's up with Ta?" he asked.

"I don't know. After he came and took the station wagon last night, I ain't see him. I went by his house this morning and nobody answered. I hope he ain't get knocked off by the police. That car should be hot by now."

"I don't know what's up with that dude lately. He aint focused," Brooklyn chided, as they now walked out of the park. He pulled his cell-phone from off his hip and called Tariq's phone but his answering service snagged the call. He hung up immediately and put the phone back on his hip. "We suppose to be getting this paper together and he out here messing with that lame D."

As they walked down Nostrand Ave, Brooklyn greeted a crew of maybe fifteen or so Bloods, who were smoking weed on the corner. They all didn't wear red as they did in other hoods like Oakland or Compton. Some had on red; others rocked black, yet others wore green, but they were all repping Blood gang.

Brooklyn wasn't a gang-banger, but he was affiliated. Being a little older than majority of the Bloods in his hood, he knew a couple of their leaders. They went to school together.

One in particular, who was among the clique, Hammer, went to High School with him and Tariq. And back in the days the three of them use to rob jewelry stores and check-cashing stores together, till they went separate ways: Brooklyn and Tariq still getting money together and Hammer got involved in the gang-life.

Brooklyn and Redd gave most of the fellas in front of the store a handshake. As they did this Redd collected a bag of weed from one of them and Brooklyn passed Hammer a ten dollar bill. "What up my G," Brooklyn said as he secretly passed him the money.

"You already know what it is, Brook," Hammer said, taking the money and sliding it into his pocket. Both Brooklyn and Redd entered the store and bought a cigar, a pack of cigarettes, and a couple of juices.

"Aiight Hammer," Brooklyn said, as him and Redd walked pass the crew on the way out of the store.

"Stay up Homie," Hammer responded. When they were a few paces away from the corner, he added, "Oh yeah, I heard about that work ya'll put in the other day." He was speaking indirectly about the robbery in front of Pedro's.

"Somebody gotta do it," Brooklyn responded quickly with a smirk as they made their way towards Gates Ave. "Like I was saying, homie, we gotta get this money," he continued his conversation with Redd. "Everybody out here eating. We gotta get focused. These clowns out here not even on our level and they putting in work out here on the streets."

As they bent a right on Gates Ave. Redd started to open the cigar, dumping its contents out on the sidewalk. They were walking towards Brooklyn's building.

"Uncle Ricky holla'd at his peeps out in P.A.," Redd said, as he poured the weed out of the bag and into the cigar paper. "They out there waiting for us as we speak." Redd licked the cigar, rolled it up, and lit it. "Ain't no time to waste, we gotta get out there and get that money," he added, as the weed he inhaled filled his throat, his lung . . . and his brain.

"Speaking of which, we gotta catch us another vic. You down for tonight?"

As Brooklyn toked on the weed, he thought about being rich, not having to depend on no one to get what he wanted. He thought about him riding through the Ave and pulling up in front of his building on a Saturday night, as the entire entourage were out there profiling, and hopping out of his brand new Range Rover, Black on Black. The girls would go crazy as he hopped out, all Gucci'd out from head to toe. He'd be the next biggest thing in the hood, even bigger than Tariq.

"You already know, I'm down," Redd added.

❋ ❋ ❋

Tariq laid in his bed, with his shades down, reading his bible. His grandmother told him to read the book of John to learn more about a real man. So he spent the entire day reading about the Lord Jesus Christ.

Tariq read and read but wasn't tired. It seemed as though he couldn't fall asleep. In fact, the more he read the more awake he became. He got stuck at one particular place. He couldn't wrap his mind around what Jesus meant when he said, "Except a corn of wheat fall into the ground and die, it abideth alone: but if it die, it bringeth forth much fruit." And "He that loveth his life shall lose it; and he that lose it his life in this world shall keep it unto life eternal." These statements touched base with him because he was beginning to hate his life, and after reading them he felt as though there may be some hope for him after all.

This was actually the first time in years that Tariq stayed home for more than two hours. Mrs. Parker began to sense that the Spirit was working on his heart, especially after her conversation with him. So she spent the entire day in the living room praying and asking God to have mercy on his tormented soul. As night fell, she knocked on his door and he was fast asleep with the Bible on his chest.

CHAPTER 27

A few days later, Faith Community Church's leadership team had gathered together in a medium size conference room. Pastor Kelly and Levi James sat at the head of a large wooden table looking embarrassed as the deacon board members, including Sherman, sat staring at them.

Sherman had on a bright, colorful suit jacket, with a loud shirt. The jacket had the four golden buttons that Mrs. Parker put in the collection plate, sewn on it in the places where other buttons had once been. He was the first to voice his opinion concerning the church's dilemma. "I tried to tell you, Daniel, but you wouldn't listen," he said.

"It's my fault," Levi responded. "I never received the initial notices that the bank swears they sent."

"Even without the notices," Marlon asked, "you didn't know that the mortgage wasn't paid?"

"I thought we had time to catch up but our members haven't been tithing like they used to," Levi defended.

"That's because they don't have it! I've been telling you that," said Sherman.

"You've made your point Sherman," responded Pastor Kelly. He was actually dealt with by the Lord all night about the entire situation. He knew he had strayed away from his calling, and had all intentions of repenting, but he waited a second too late. He didn't think it would happen just yet. But yet he was thankful because it could have been worse. So he cried out to the Lord, sought forgiveness, and called the meeting so he can confess his faults to his leadership. "All the blame I squarely place at my own feet. I've been distracted, taking God for granted. I thought he would always provide, and I wasn't handling my responsibilities. I squandered the Lord's money on exorbitant payrolls, and things that don't benefit our church and its members. And I know that the Lord isn't please."

"Are you in any position at all to save the church?" asked Anthony.

"No!" Pastor Kelly responded, putting his head down.

Just as he said this someone knocked at the door.

"Yes, come in," said the pastor.

Karen Kelly opened the door and entered, followed by Mrs. Parker, April, Donteer, and Mildred. Everyone was dressed in black, except for Mrs. Kelly, who held a piece of paper in her hand. The pastor and deacons looked at them confused.

"They asked to speak with you and the deacons," said Karen to Pastor Kelly.

"Are you wearing black because of the church's affairs?" the pastor asked trying to lighten the mood. "Because if you are, you don't have to be so dramatic."

"We just came from a funeral," Mildred responded. "A dear friend was laid to rest."

"I'm sorry. I meant no offense."

"I know," she continued. "We came by because we heard about the church's financial situation, and we're concerned."

"Again I apologize to you, Mrs. Parker. And the Browns, both of you have been very good members. I don't know what else to say."

Mildred then responded. "How about, I've learned a great deal from this experience and I will lead this church with new zest and zeal."

"I am sorry, Mrs. Brown, but I don't think that you understand fully what's going on. There will be no more Faith Community. The bank is foreclosing our building being that we weren't able to keep up on our monthly payments." There was a moment of silence before the pastor continued. "You know what, I'm sorry—all of you," he apologized once again. "There's no one else to blame in all this, but myself. I have been a very bad example of what a leader is supposed to be."

Levi tried to share some of the blame. "It's not your . . ."

But Pastor Kelly cut him off. "Levi, please, I must do this," he continued. "The Lord is chastising me." He then turned to Levi. "I've set a very bad example for you," he told him. Then he looked over at Sherman. "And Sherman, you were right all along. I hope you can find it in your heart to forgive me for all those things I said." The Pastor then turned his attention to everyone. "All of you. Please forgive me. I'm truly sorry."

Mrs. Parker responded immediately. She saw that he was truly broken, and repentful about his actions. "If you had the money," she asked him, "Would you restore Faith Community to its prior glory?" Before he could answer, she continued. "I would like to see it go back to how it was when me and Earnest first joined, when Faith Community was fully dedicated to the reverence of the Lord, when there was unity, love, and respect among all of God's children." She then looked to Sherman, who responded nodding his head. Mrs. Parker then spoke back to Pastor Kelly. "Then use my gifts," she added, pointing to Sherman's jacket, "that I have given to the church. It should be more than enough."

Pastor Kelly, Levi, and all of the deacons looked confused. Sherman looked and touched the buttons on his jacket. "You mean these ornamental things?"

Pastor Kelly looked exhausted. He thought the woman was trying his patience. "Mrs. Parker, thank you, but your tokens will not help." But his wife, Karen, helped to clarify what was going on.

"Dear, they're not worthless tokens. Mrs. Parker explained to me that the buttons are actual gold coins that date back to biblical days." She walked over to her husband and handed him a piece of paper with a gold seal on it. "This is a sign of authenticity," she said.

As Pastor Kelly read it, Sherman stood up and everyone stared at the golden buttons on his jacket. The Pastor looked up at him, and then got everyone's attention.

"Thank you Lord," he said looking up. "Let's all pray."

❋ ❋ ❋

On the way home, Donteer drove and April was in the passenger seat. Mrs. Parker was in the back seat, next to Mildred, who turned to Mrs. Parker and shared her appreciation.

"Your benevolence is amazing, Mrs. Parker," said Mildred.

"I've always done what the Lord has told me," Mrs. Parker responded. "About a month ago, He told me to give those artifacts to the church, even before I learned of its financial problems."

"Yes, I know. But it would've been hard for me to give them away when I think about how valuable they are, that they were the same pieces of gold handled by Jacob."

"We need Faith Community to go on, because I've seen it save so many souls. The coins are valuable but a soul is priceless."

* * *

After the incident with Mark, Keesha was a bit depressed. She really liked him, and was hoping that she did the right thing. She needed a little encouragement, and who better to call than her friend Kim. If nothing else, she could definitely count on her to be candid.

Kim was in her room reading a fashion magazine when the phone rang.

"Hello?" she answered.

"Hey, what are you doing?" Keesha asked.

"Reading a magazine. What's up?"

"My parents went to a family friend's funeral. My grandfather is watching us."

"What happened with Mark?" Kim asked smiling, as if she couldn't wait for all the juicy details.

"He was lying to me. I caught him. He couldn't even look me in the eye. And he began to stutter, so I left."

"Wow, that was smart of you."

"Yeah, it was, wasn't it? I liked myself for that."

CHAPTER 28

"It's been a crazy week," Donteer told April, as they laid in bed, her head resting on his chest. They both were reflecting on the week.

"I know," April concurred.

"When will they know the results of your follow-up exams?" Donteer asked.

"In a day or two they're gonna call."

"I know everything will be fine. I've seen a lot of God's grace in the last few days alone. Me and Abler visited over a dozen people, and every message, every package, every word of encouragement that he gave the people was amazing."

"I can imagine. There is something about him," said April, thinking about her dream. "I can feel it. I can't put it into words. He's almost . . ."

Donteer knew exactly what his wife was thinking. " . . . ethereal," he completed her thought.

* * *

Just that quick Donteer's life was changed. Abler came and left, leaving a profound effect on the rest of the family. After he left, Donteer admitted to April that he actually missed his presence.

The next week everyone in the Brown family were a little better off than they were before Abler came but they hardly noticed it, that is, except for Donteer. He noticed the difference between him and April's relationship. It was a bit more peaceful, and April's faith grew. Every night before they went to sleep they would read the Bible to each other. Leonard even began to pray.

❋ ❋ ❋

Early the following Saturday morning, in front of the Brown's home, Jamal was dressed in a sweat suit, waiting for Biz and Pooh. He'd been waiting for this moment all week. One way or another, he knew he had to handle his business. He worked out, but he also prayed, and prayed a few more times while waiting for that day.

As he leaned up against his father's car, for the first time Jamal wasn't fearful. He felt confident and ready for whatever.

Biz and Pooh walked up moments later, and stopped in front of him. Biz was the first to set it off.

"Where you been at? I've been looking for you," he asked Jamal.

"My family had some personal things going on, so I had to be there for them." He was still leaning up against the car when he said this, then he stood straight up in

Biz's face. "I'm here now. What you want?" he asked him, looking in his face.

Biz sensed a whole new aura coming from Jamal's presence. "Why are you talking like that?" he asked Jamal, looking at him from head to toe.

"Like what?" Jamal said, still looking in his face, now gazing into his eyes.

"Like you tough?" said Biz in a serious tone, tightening his face.

"I'm not tough Biz, I'm just talking," he responded calmly.

Biz looked at Jamal intensely, as Jamal continued to stare into his eyes. Biz then turned and looked at Pooh, who was anxious to speak. "You sound like you got some new base in your voice," Pooh cut in.

"Whatever," Jamal said, brushing him off while still staring at Biz.

Jamal then remembered what Abler had told him. He realized he didn't have to be scared, or even act tough, because God has his back. And he felt as though God was standing right there with him. He then decided to take control of the situation. "I don't want no problems with you Biz," he said calmly, then looked at Pooh, "or you Pooh. But I don't want to be your friend either," he continued. "I don't think we have the same things in common."

"Me either," Biz answered immediately. He realized that he really didn't want Jamal as an underling. He was beginning to speak his mind already, Biz thought. He also realized that Jamal was a leader, and a potential threat to him in the future. "But you know what," he continued, "I don't need no more friends, so forget you. I was just messing with you anyway." He gave Pooh a pound and they walked off laughing, as Jamal walked into the house.

❋ ❋ ❋

Inside, Donteer, Leonard, April, Mildred, Keesha, and Kim were all hiding in the dark, looking out several windows, peeping from their corners. When they saw him coming back into the house everyone ran and acted nonchalant as if they didn't know what was going on outside.

Donteer sat down and picked up a book. April grabbed a magazine. Leonard and Mildred grabbed some playing cards, pretending to be playing. And Keesha and Kim sat on the floor, staring at a movie on the television. Jamal walked in and was first greeted by his dad.

"Hey, what's up?" said Donteer.

"It went okay, but you know that. I saw somebody in the window."

"Window?" Donteer responded, trying his best to hold a straight face.

"Dad, I saw several curtains move. You told."

"He better had told," said April, trying to help Donteer out. "I don't want you out there fighting, Jamal."

"Mom, I was standing up for myself," he said.

Of the entire family, Donteer understood the most what Jamal was going through. Even though situations were different during his childhood days, Donteer could still relate to his plight, being a young black man growing up in the hood, and trying not to succumb to its pressures. His son was following in his footsteps, and he was proud.

"April it worked," Donteer said with a cool and confident smile. "Let's be proud of the boy."

Everyone looked at Jamal, filled with a sense of pride. Keesha and Kim went over and kissed him on the cheek. His face lit up, filled with even more confidence in himself, reassured that standing up against peer-pressure was the right thing to do.

* * *

Back at the corner store, several young fellas were off to the side of the bodega shooting dice. Most of them were younger than Tariq's age, but older than Biz and Pooh. A few of them were Bloods; both young men and women. They were around Brooklyn and Redd, who were still enjoying their five minutes of fame from the Robbery on the corner, and a few more recent exploits. They were waiting to holla at Tariq about their scheduled trip that night.

Brooklyn and Redd were ready to make their move to Pennsylvania. They had a little over ten thousand dollar and were ready to cop the drugs to take with them. Since they tried to contact Tariq and he never answered or returned their calls, they continued with their plans business as usual. They hadn't seen him since he came to pick up the station wagon from Redd. He had called them that morning and told them to meet him on the corner. They still didn't get a chance to speak to him because he was busy talking to someone on the other side of the street. They talked to a couple of girls while they waited.

Tariq stood on the other side of the corner looking down the block as Biz and Pooh walked his way. They looked apprehensive as they approached.

"Did ya'll little dudes do what I said?" Tariq asked them.

Pooh shook his head nervously, as Biz responded. "Yeah Tariq."

"Aiight! Don't bother that kid no more, or I'ma bother ya'll."

Tariq then crossed the street to where Brooklyn and Redd were standing, talking to the couple girls. "Yo Brook, Redd, let me holla at ya'll," Tariq said, as he approached.

The way he spoke alerted the girls that they were imposing, so they left. But not before one of them, Trisha, who was talking to Redd, smiled and said, "Hi Tariq."

"Trish, what up ma," Tariq responded and then turned his attention back to Brooklyn and Redd. "Yo, I been doing some thinking about that outta town move. That's not where I'm at right now."

"So where you at right now homie, because . . ." Brooklyn attempted to cut in, clearly angry but Tariq held his hand up at Brooklyn.

"Chill out let me finish what I'm saying champ." Brooklyn reached into his pocket, pulled out a pack of Newports and lit one as Tariq continued. "Ya'll my dudes, and I thought the least I should do is give you an explanation, and that's why I'm here now." Both Brooklyn and Redd listened intently to what Tariq was about to say. "I been out here for years wasting my life, and honestly homies, your lives too and all these other lil dudes lives that be out here looking up to me." The more he spoke the more the corner got quiet. "I'm tired of being out here burning down my own hood. I'm tired of hustling out here, shooting dudes, and sell crack to my neighbors, my peoples, and their families and friends. Trust me, I thought about this long and hard. That ain't what my purpose in life is. It's bigger than destroying, it's about building back." As Tariq spoke about his purpose, Brooklyn figured it had something to do with Donteer.

"Ta, I don't know what happened to you in the past couple weeks, but I'm not tryna figure it out. Me and Redd got ten gs right now to cop, with or without you." If Brooklyn knew Tariq well enough, he understood that Tariq knew that money talks. And so he decided against listening to all this Obama talk about change, and building and all that, and appealed to Tariq's love for money. "We got a spot waiting for us right now in P.A., waiting for us to come and blow it up.

Tariq thought for a second. He was definitely tempted. Here it was, they had ten thousand dollars and was practically begging him to give him some. Any other day he would have came up with a way to benefit off of their share without even putting in his own. But he thought also about all his homies that left and never came back. He thought about how reckless Brooklyn and Redd were getting, even making him hot. He thought about his grandmother, about his boy Donteer, and his future, about being a true hustler and making the best out of his already bad situation, and this time he would do it the right way. "Nah," he concluded. "I'm good. I'ma hold it down out here."

Brooklyn was clearly frustrated. "What ya'll clowns looking at," he said to the group of Bloods who were listening to their conversation not too far from where they were standing. They then looked away and resumed their conversation.

Brooklyn and Redd had put that work in. They'd been on a little robbing spree to get their money up. And, to Brooklyn, everything was still going according to plans, even without Tariq. This wasn't even a minor set-back, he thought. Actually, he was prepared to go out of town by himself if he had too. But honestly, the last thing he had expected to hear was that Tariq was trying to change his life. He thought the reason why he didn't hear from Tariq was because he didn't have his share of money. Or, maybe he didn't want to leave the hood because he still had money floating around on the corner. But as he thought about this whole talk about change, it began to rouse him up. He then poked at Tariq's ego.

"Yo Ta, you disappointed me, Son," Brooklyn chided. "That's all I want you to know. Sound like you been drinking that same holy water that ya man D been drinking. But it's all good," he added. "When I see you again, I'ma buy you a bottle of Crystal, that real stuff."

Redd laughed. Even Tariq had to smile at Brooklyn's sarcasm, thinking to himself, this fool don't know no better. He's lucky I'm trying to change my life.

"I don't know about you, kid," Brooklyn continued. "But I aint got time to waste out here. I gotta get food, and put clothes on my back, oh . . . and cop nice Range for the summer. We'll holla at you. Have fun with your white man's religion," he ended abruptly. He looked at Redd and they both left immediately without even as much as shaking Tariq's hand. They had moves to make.

Tariq stood there leaning up against a car just thinking as they left. It was a tough decision to make . . . to leave all of the past behind him. Even the way Brooklyn talked to him. But in the past week he had turned a new chapter in his life. He had gave his heart to Jesus Christ. The old things and the old man were fading away, and all things were becoming new. “Stay up,” he said to himself, and to Brooklyn and Redd as they disappeared up the block.

CHAPTER 29

Donteer was back on the search for employment. Now he was beginning to feel a little more faithful in the Lord with all the events that had taken place. But as he walked into the house one day that following week April ran into his arms crying.

"What is it?" he questioned, searching his mind nervously to find out what can it possibly be. She was so excited that she couldn't even talk for a moment. But eventually, when she calmed down she sat him down on a nearby couch and broke the news to him.

"The test came back negative," she said smiling. "No more signs of cancer. And baby, it was the Lord that healed me."

Donteer was so thrilled that he picked her up on impulse and spun her around, as tears flowed from his eyes. "Thank you Lord," he said out loud, in a rapture of emotions. "I love you," he said both to the Lord and to his wife.

April felt as though she owed so much to him for the many times she was weak, wanting to give up, but he kept her strong. She loved him ten thousand times more as he spun her around in his arms. The entire family then came out into the living room and partook in one big group hug. And everyone's faith in the Lord grew a hundredfold.

❋ ❋ ❋

The following Sunday would be one to remember, as April, Donteer, Mildred, Jamal, and Keesha, were all dressed in their Sunday best to go offer praises unto the Lord for all the great things he had done. As they walked to the car, Leonard walked out of the house all dressed up. Everyone turned around and looked at him as if they saw a ghost.

"What?" he responded to their stares, walking towards his car.

Mildred knew that with God all things were possible, but clearly the Lord had outdone Himself with this one, she thought. "You're going to church with us?" she asked him.

"No, not this week. But I want to drive you there so get in my car," he told her. He then handed his wife the keys to his car, which was parked behind Donteer's car. She got in, as April and the kids got into Donteer's. Donteer stopped to talk with his father.

"You're just gonna drive mom and come back home?" he asked smiling but somewhat confused.

"No, I'll wait outside for her, and bring her back."

"I don't understand, dad."

"I'm trying Donteer. That's all there is to understand."

He hated to burst their bubble but, reality was, it took a lot for him to even be seen on Sunday, driving to church, with church clothes on. But God . . . was chipping away at his pride. Donteer knew that and hugged his dad.

❋ ❋ ❋

Inside of Faith Community Church, Pastor Kelly addressed the congregation from up front. "Brothers, Sisters," he began. "Our church has just made it through some very difficult times, with the help of one of our oldest members—Sister Abigal Parker." He pointed to her. "We are deeply grateful. Sister Parker has given so very much, that her benevolence has birth a new passion in me. Today, we will not be taking up any collections, nor will we for some time to come." In a pew close to the front, Donteer was squeezing April's hands. Next to them were Mildred and the kids. Pastor Kelly continued. "We will be doing some reverse tithing for a while, in effort to assist the many members of our congregation that fell into difficult financial times."

Several of the church members responded, "Praise the Lord."

The Pastor continued. "The reverse tithe was an idea from a new member-Brother Donteer Brown." He pointed to Donteer, while many members acknowledged him with smiles. "Brother Brown is out of work, and God saw fit to use him to generate many solid ideas to help us out. He also has a degree in Business. With so many members of our church owning businesses, I can't see Mr. Brown not being offered a job."

Some members turned and offered Donteer their cards.

As Donteer thanked those who passed him their cards, he looked in the back and saw Abler sitting in the last pew. He was dressed in all white, looking handsome and very clean, without a mark on his face. He was sitting next to Trisha Truepenny.

"Excuse me, honey!" Donteer said turning to April, while Pastor Kelly continued to address the congregation.

He stood up and went to where Abler sat. Abler was gone. Donteer looked down and saw a beautifully bonded white Bible on the seat next to Trisha, who looked beautiful, and years younger. She smiled and greeted Donteer.

"Hello, Mr. Brown. I didn't know you attend this church."

"I just started attending regularly. What can I say, God has been good to me. And yourself . . . how have you been?"

Trisha couldn't hold her tongue. She bubbled over with joy, and began sharing her testimony with Donteer right there during service, as the pastor's sermon faded out. "I feel like a new person. He's definitely shined his light into my life. Just a couple weeks ago I was at a dark moment in my life. My husband left me while I was pregnant, then my daughter died. I really couldn't see any reason to live. But I cried out to God, asking him for a sign to live. I didn't hear anything and was about to kill myself. Right at the moment that I was about to kill myself, I saw someone at my door. And when I answered it, a man, a total stranger, came and told me that the Lord has heard my prayers, and that my daughter was in heaven. He spoke like a angel. Each word that came from his mouth felt as though it added life to my life. And, as if that wasn't good enough, I woke up this morning and felt the need to go to church only to hear that you guys are doing the reverse tithing. Lord knows I need it—thanks to you."

"Wow, that's amazing Ms. Truepenny." As he thought about everything she said, and then about Abler, he inquired about him. He could've sworn he just saw him. "Excuse me," he intervened, "but was someone sitting here beside you a few seconds ago?"

"No," she responded. "I've been sitting here by myself since the service began."

Wow, this can't be happening, Donteer thought to himself. He knew it was something special about Abler, but it couldn't be what he was thinking, an angel? He looked around in wonder, then looked down at the Bible sitting next to her.

"Is this your Bible?" he asked Ms. Truepenny.

"No, actually it's just been sitting there."

Donteer reached down to pick up the Bible and a business card fell out. He picked it up and read it. The card read:

In my book, you are a Good Samaritan,

I've put a good word in with my Boss.

Abler Pen;

Heaven Sent.

Donteer looked at the Bible and then looked up at the Pastor Kelly, still addressing the congregation. Pastor Kelly's voice faded again as Donteer caught a sudden flashback of Abler. In the flashback, Abler was in the guest room, in the tee shirt that read 'DOG'. He was facing the mirror over the dresser as Donteer was behind him. The reflection in the mirror showed Abler without any bruises or injuries, almost glowing. Again he was smiling. And this time his tee shirt read 'GOD'.

Donteer shook his head, almost in unbelief but then smiled to himself. It really happened, he thought. I entertained an angel. And I'm in church.

He was stuck in time for a few moments thinking about everything, totally oblivious to the people that walked pass and thanked him. He shot pass them, running outside into the middle of the streets. He looked up and saw a bright light moving in the sky and just knew it was Abler.

"Thank you Lord," Donteer said out loud, as his voice rang out loud beyond the clouds and into heaven.

EPILOGUE

A new dawn is on the rise, in which socialism is slowly being inculcated in the minds of our people. The economic downturn has turned up some misplaced values in our homes, institutions, communities, and our governments. For the past century, some pockets of the world, especially the United States and the United Kingdom, have flourished economically, while our Godly values have plummeted. We have turned our backs on our fellow man right beside us. And, becoming so engulfed in our material and naturalistic ideals, the essential element of the Supernatural has slowly faded from our minds. At least some of us.

Donteer was an exception. Although he never saw Abler again, he always remembered every moment he shared with the Heaven Sent messenger. Every chance he had, Donteer shared his testimony of his encounter with an angel. He reminded others to always extend a helping hand to strangers, because you may well be entertaining angels—angels who were sent by God to help us. His household, church, and practically all of his neighborhood was impacted spiritually by just one act of goodness. Even Tariq began attending church with his grandmother.

Unfortunately, Brooklyn was killed in a shootout in Pennsylvania, in which Redd was wounded. Redd was so shook up by the incident that, with Tariq's help, he decided to change his life. Furthermore, Tariq felt a calling to go into the ministry, giving his life fully to the Lord, even willing to die for what is right. Grandma Parker was so proud that she used the rest of her savings to put him through Seminary School. And exactly one year later, she went home to be with the Lord, while Tariq went on to serve the Lord as a youth pastor, helping to change hundreds, even thousands of lives in his hood ministry.

Thus, with this new era ensuing, men and women of God; of all color, conviction, and creed, need to be extremely attentive to what Jesus Christ is unfolding for us to see. All power in heaven and earth is still in His hands. Let us not be overwhelmed by the media and other mediums of information but let us incline our ears to His voice through obedience to His Word and Spirit. Even socialists' ideals can be used to help us take our eyes off the material and look to the spiritual, from the natural back to the Supernatural. And with the Lord's help, even socialism can be a helpful platform, upsurging some misplaced essential Christian values such as loving thy neighbor as thyself. For though economic bubbles may burst, and the stock market tumble and crumble, the Word of God will continue to stand firm, upholding the hearts and minds of the faithful—until He comes.

TALKING POINTS

1. From the character initially seen in Donteer, did you think he would end up in prison? What does this tell us about the nature of circumstances young men and women face daily that can land them in prison? Is there any other way that Donteer could have dealt with that situation? If so, how?

2. Do you think God was the one who put Donteer in prison to have him saved? Or, was it Donteer's own decision that resulted in the consequence of a prison sentence?

3. During the time of Christ, Samaritans were people who were out casted from society. In what ways were Donteer ostracized? In the parable of the Good Samaritan, a Levite and a priest walked past their neighbor, who was left to die on the road. In what ways do the "religious" people of today turn their backs on their neighbors? What do you think contributes the most to such

spiritual blindness? What ideas do you have to help your neighbor in order to overcome such spiritual blindness.

4. At what point did you realize that Abler came from heaven? Keep it real! Do you think there was anything significant about Donteer's character that God saw fit to send an angel to visit him and his family? Biblically, what role do angels play in our lives? (Heb. 1:14)

5. Do you think demonic forces are as active in adolescents' lives as they are in the lives of adults? If you answered no, clearly you haven't been in the hood. Besides Abler, who or what else do you think played a role in Jamal and Keesha being less susceptible to the influence of evil forces?

6. Do you think church leaders are more or less susceptible to the influences of evil forces? Why do you think Satan would want to target those in church leadership? Being a man of God, endowed with His Spirit and gifted with understanding spiritual things, why do you think that Satan was so successful in tempting Pastor Kelly? Do you think you should care if a pastor or a church leader is genuinely a man of God, led by His Spirit? Or, we shouldn't judge?
7. Do you think it was coincidence that Tariq came just when Donteer and Abler was in his house? In the hood, do you think that a lot of the senseless murders derive from demonic—motivated

thoughts? How much do you think a person's upbringing has to do with him or her getting caught up in the streets? If you have any kids, or are planning to have any, how would you prevent your kids from becoming victims of the devil's traps in the hood?

8. Do you think it's fair that Christians die from terrible sicknesses, such as cancer, when the Holy Spirit that God gives us is able to heal us? Considering Sheila's life, do you think anything good can come about from a Christian that has such ailments? Do you think they come from God, the devil, or just as a result of our human imperfection? What do you think was the lesson learned from God healing one believer and letting the other die from the same illness?

9. Overall, what do you think was the message, or messages, Donteer taught us with his one act of goodness to help Abler? As a result, what do we learn about God as we obey His Word? How can you imitate Donteer in laying down your neighbor as he did, in your everyday life?

10. Abler appeared to Trisha Truepenny's house right when she was about to take her own life. With all that happened to Abler on his way to deliver his message to her, what does this say about God's timing? How does this encourage you if you're waiting right now on the Lord to answer a prayer or to step in on a specific situation?

HERE'S A PREVIEW FROM: THE HOOD SHEPHERD

PROLOGUE

"I can't believe that you may be getting a record deal," Monigue said, speaking to her arrogant and possessive boyfriend, Max.

Maximillian Davis was his real name. Mad Max was his street handle and rap signature, not only because the moniker went well his name, but also because it mirrored his sometimes deranged personality. To Monique, however, who'd been dating him for up to a year prior, Max was just . . . . Max.

"Well believe it!" Max quickly spat, pushing his midnight colored, cromed-out, BMW 745 to its capacity through downtown Atlanta. "I'm waiting for the call-back now. Jimmy said a lotta labels are interested. But he tryna get me to change my name from Mad Max. I don't know about that."

Max had been an independent rap artist, moving his own units for a little over a year. And Monique had to admit, he'd done well for himself. He'd picked up a nice car and a decent pad in Dekalb County. Of course, this was with his manager, Jimmy Owen's, help. It was the light skinned and heavy set, bald and fast talking manager who had shown Max how to work the streets and the internet to promote himself, pushing out street Utube videos of his battles like every week. And in each of those videos Max would push the envelope, coming at some popular artist, also inciting them to a battle. It didn't take long at all before the name Mad Max started buzzing and popping, spreading like virtual wildfires.

At this time, Jimmy was prepping Max to take his game to a whole nother level, as Jimmy would tell it. He was having possible talks with CEOs, possibly even able to land Max his very own label under one of the fastest growing labels in the south, Cocaine Records.

While listening to Max talk, Monique thought for a second how crazy her twenty-sixth year with the rapper had been, but then concluded that it had been a year at the beach compared to the rest of her life, especially after hearing the good news about him possibly setting his foot in the door. Good thing she hung in there, she told herself, also feeling a sense of accomplishment for putting up with his crazy self. Now all of their problems will soon be washed away. "You started recording the month we started dating, right?" she asked him.

"Yeah, but I was always in the streets grinding, battling cats at underground jams. Never even lost one. I had these dudes scared to death to battle me. The industry might be late in catching wind of who I am but, trust me, these dudes out here know what time it is."

As he spoke, Max noticed Monique steadily fixing her make-up in the mirror from his peripheral. With her full-body fire blonde-colored hair twisting and twirling a little past her shoulders, which accentuated her bronze skin tone, Max always told her that she reminded him of Beyonce, with a cute little distinguishable mole on her left cheek which set her apart as his chick. To him, her knockout body was only a plus, a plus that he'd appreciated very much, thank you. Of all the Women Max had dealt with, Monique was totally in a class by herself. As she was his very own calender chick. AS she touched herself up in the mirror, it was clear to Max that his girl, Monique Love was bad . . . and she knew it.

Pulling up to the stoplight, Max eyed her as she guided the lipgloss lightly onto her lips. A few more seconds went by, then he spoke again. "Why does it seem like you're tryna look extra cute today?"

She licked her lips, snapped shut the compact mirror, pulled down her Christian Dior sunglasses over her face, then glanced one more time into the passenger side of the rear view mirror before she responded. "Ain't nobody trying to look extra anything!" She then turned to face him as the car was moving again and he was refocused on the road. "And I don't like the way you said that!" she added.

"Why?" he asked, not even bothering to look over at her.

"Because it implies that I didn't look extra cute yesterday."

That made him glance over at her, as she wore an extra cute smile. "Yeah, I hear that!" he said, as he continued to focus on the road.

A few seconds later, Max pulled up to the curb right in front of Monique's job for the past six months, 'Get In Where You Fit In Books.' She then cozied up to him. "I'm just playing with you, baby" she said, leaning over and kissing him lightly on his lips, which he returned. "You know I only look cute for you," she added, smiling.

"You better!" was his response.

"Whateva!" she spat back. "Are you coming to pick me up?" she asked him. "Or should I take the bus home?"

"Today's one of them days, babe. Take the bus. I'll be home later."

"You mean to tell me that you're going to let . . ." Monique sassily ran her index fingers down the contour of her body. " . . . All of this ride on public transportation."

Max had to admit, she did look temptimg sitting there in an incandescent orange cargo dress that gracefully hugged her curves and short enough to reveal her golden thighs, with sandals matching her orange leather satchel. She looked hot. "Mo, everybody in the 'A' know that you're Mad Max's orange crush, crushing em just the same way I'ma be crushing these dudes in the booth. So all of that," he said, gesturing to her body, "betta be home, and fully in-tact, when I get back, or I'ma lay down the smack," he added, rapping in a serious tone.

"Please," she countered. "This ain't no 106 and Park. If you gonnakick some rap to me, you better step your game up," she added. "Cause that stuff you talking sound wack," she said, smiling and opening the door.

"Yeah aiiight!" Max responded nonchalantly.

As Monique was about to ease herself out of the car, Max's Blackberry rang. He ignored it, as he did sometimes to make her feel special. "Mo, call me at lunch," he told her, not even looking at his phone.

"Max, we don't always take lunch. It's just me and Ms. Tahlisa. Sometimes we work right through."

"You heard what I said?" he spat.

Ooooh, who are you talking to like that, was what ran through her mind, but she didn't dare say that. She knew he was serious by the look in his eyes. She had to let him shine. He was definitely feeling himself and she was feeling good, so why spoil that with some petty argument? Besides, she had learned to embrace his darker side. Even from the first day she met him it was hard for him to hide. Sure, he was a fine black brother, brown skin, with waves spinning out of control. He had to be somebody, she remembered thinking, or on his way to becoming somebody, the way he swagged, like he owned the sidewalk, and with a cute baby face that she still could not resist. She could work with him, Monique thought as he approached, looking like Carmelo Anthony without the tattoos. She chose him, she reminded herself as she stared into those serious eyes, just like Lala chose Carmelo.

Monique huffed, then responded with a quick, "Alright," and exited the car.

Before she could even make it three full steps, Max's 745 looked late as it was once again meandering through the bustling early morning traffic on Peach Tree Street, with his cellphone glued to his ear. Monique kept it moving, confident that he was late for the studio or for a meeting with his manager, Jimmy. He better be, she thought, trying her very best to trust him after all they had been through.

Things were finally looking up for them and their future, she told herself, choosing to remain optimistic as she held her head high, shining as bright as the beautiful sun that pierced the clouds on that momentus day.

CHAPTER 2

When Monique opened the door to the bookstore, where she worked as a sales clerk, the light from the sun receded back as she entered and noticed her boss. "Morning, Ms. Tahlisa," she greeted cordially, taking her sunglasses off and closing the door gently behind her.

Tahlisa Mitchell was thirty-two years old, very pretty and sophisticated looking, of average weight and height. She had a very zestful personality. This was why Monique could immediately sense that something was wrong with her. With her shades off now, Monique could still sense that the atmosphere in the store was dark and gloomy because it was written all over her boss's face.

"Good Morning, Monique," Ms. Tahlisa Mitchell greeted back in a serious tone. "I need to talk to you before you get settled."

Just that quick, Monique's mind went from zero to sixty, methodically scanning through all of her job responsibilities from the previous day, and from the previous week, since it was already Friday.

Okay, she wasn't late—check. In fact, she was ten minutes early, as she was most of the times. She had organized each bookshelf of each genre of urban literature, each according to category, author, and then aphalbetical order—check. She had made sure all the books were neat and orderly, not turned upside down or inside out, as most customers would haphazardly leave books and magazines in disarray. Check, check, check. Everything should be in order, she told herself.

Maybe it's the inventory, Monique then considered. Usually every other Friday, her boss would go in the back to begin on the inventory and she needed Monique to run the check -in counter. With her clerical experience, she was also able to work the computer or cash register if necessary. Maybe that's it, she concluded, as she approached the counter where Ms. Tahlisa Mitchell stood.

"Is everything all right?" Monique asked her.

"I'm afraid not," she responded.

Monique walked behind the counter, resting her pocket-book down as she listened to her boss.

"You've helped me so much, Monique, and I thank you. But 'Get In' books is a small business and I can't afford you anymore, not in this economy."

Oh no. This . . . can't . . . be . . . happening. Especially not after . . . "But, Ms. Tahlisa, book sales are picking up. People are gravitating to this inexpensive source on entertainment," she offered.

"Not fast enough. And certainly not with Ebooks outselling the traditional paperback and hardcover books. I'm sorry, Monique. Really, I am, but I have to watch my expenses," she added, candidly. "Maybe when business picks back up you can come back. I can give you this week's pay. I'll be right back."

Ms. Tahlisa Mitchell walked into the back room as Monique stood behind the counter trying to recover. She felt like she just fell, or rather like someone had just pushed her twenty stories to the ground. And then like she was deflated by one of those eighteen wheeler trucks. She still couldn't pick herself back up. Still dazed, she just stared at the books on the shelves until her boss came back out, walked over and gave her an envelope and a hug. "Take care," she added. "And keep reading."

Keep reading. She fires me then she wants to be Maya Angelou, Monique thought to herself. But she simply replied, "I will," snatched her pocketbook from the counter and walked towards the door.

Monique didn't say anything else. She couldn't. She felt betrayed, like someone had just stabbed her in the back. She just couldn't believe what just had happened. After she had devoted herself in the past six months to helping her boss build her business, being that it was a start-up business when she first started working there, sometimes even working way past the designated work hours, and at other times even opening up to her about her past and also about her relationship with Max, how he cheated on her with some nasty stripper and how she found out because her best friend also had a cousin who was a stripper at the same club. When she found out and was about to leave, he begged her not to leave because he really needed her. Furthermore, Monique also told her how Max didn't even want her to work at some bookstore, but that she felt she had to have a separate identity from his. Of course, she felt betrayed, and humiliated. Painstakenly, however, she tried her best to pick herself up off the floor and move on.

* * *

Once again, Monique thought as she left, the world had let her down. But this wasn't anything new. This was the story of her life. She'd tried her very best to look beyond her past, beyond her painful experience of being abandoned by her mother to an orphanage from the age of three. Guess she had more important things to tend to. From there she was moved from orphanage to orphanage and then from group home to group home. She'd look beyond the hurt and humiliation of being molested in those group homes—which Monique called grope homes—her reward for being pretty and overdeveloped from a young age. She had even looked pass being raped in her last group home at the age of sixteen, and by then she was so used to being abused and mistreated that she literally picked herself up, dusted herself off, and kept moving. Literally, as though she fell and bruised an arm or leg or something, without shedding as much as a tear. And this was what she tried to do on this dreary day. She pulled herself together and kept it moving.

Guess Max was right, she pondered further, as she made her way up Peach Tree, still convincing herself that she was a Georgia Peach. He was really all she had and she was his Georgia Peach. True, their relationship had been rocky, but it was also true that they had weathered the storm together. He always told her: they had a special bond and shared a similar past which brought them together, and which will keep them together. And though Max had cheated on her once, he had convinced her that he would change, and that, being that they were meant to be together, she was placed in his heart to help change his life, and vice versa. She suddenly felt the need to be comforted by him.

Monique stopped walking and rifled through her pocketbook, pulling out her Blackberry and keying in Max's number. No answer. Guess he was still busy, she figured, hanging up the phone without leaving a message. She definitely didn't feel like talking to no answering service. She simply hit him with a text—KUTGW—encouraging him to keep up the good work; and—TOY—letting him know that she was thinking of him.

On her way to the bus stop, Monique spent another fifteen minutes or so window shopping with the rest of the patrons on Peach Tree Street, just trying to get her mind off the fact that she was just laid off. This was a mental defense mechanism she had developed over time to deal with all the harsh realities of life, especially a life like her's. She had simply willed herself not to think about the bad by telling herself good things, about all the finer things in life. And, for her, it had worked. Really, what was finer than shopping? Or, in her case, window shopping? Only thing she knew finer than that was herself, she thought, as she looked at her reflection in the window of a shoe store. After all that she had went through, look how beautiful she was. Her man certainly thought so, splurging on her every chance he got. Almost everything she had within the past year or so, Max had bought for her. She hated getting into fights with him but she had to admit, dude really knew how to make up. As she thought about him she decided to head home. Monique waited for another ten minutes by the bus stop and then boarded a bus to Dekalb County.

CHAPTER 3

While on the bus, amid the gawks and smiles from strangers, both men and women, Monique couldn't help thinking about Max and his crazy behind. She had definitely grew to love him like an acquired taste. Their meeting each other couldn't have been more perfect, she reminisced. His timing and his swagger was impeccable. She had just broken up with, uhm, what's his name, oh, Shawn the cop.

Fresh out the academy, this fool was off the hook. He was the wrong person to give a gun to. He took his job way too serious, rolling up on guys smoking weed while they were together. Another time he tried to pull his gun out on some stranger who had looked at her too long. Off the hook. He hadn't come to terms yet with the fact that his girl was bad, and that, no matter what she did or where she went, she would attract the attention of other men. When he did seem to understand that, he tried to lock her down.

That was the wrong move.

He became way too controlling and tried way too hard. He literally didn't want her to leave the house.

Don't ever back a woman like her into the corner, Monique often said, or she will get out. And he had the nerve to ask her to have his kids, with an 's'. Oh no, that was it. This fool literally thought he was going to have her stay home all day making babies, while he went out acting like he was the man because he had his bad, exotic—looking chick on lock down. He definitely had it twisted. He must've been smoking crack because he had the wrong one. Somebody should have told him that. But he let her slip right through his hand when Max swagged by and snagged her up.

Now Max . . . was Monique's savior and didn't even know it. At the time she was working as a secretary at a small insurance company selling Universal Insurance, only a few blocks from the 'Get In' bookstore, and she was on her lunch break at Gladys Knight's Chicken and Waffle restaurant. She loved their food, and its outdoor atmosphere right there in the center of all the action on Peach Tree.

As Monique sat by herself enjoying the breeze that kissed her face on that balmy day while reading a Chicken Soup book, she heard the sounds of Waka Flaka's, 'I go hard in the Paint,' pumping through someone's Bazooka car speakers, which rattled the table her food was on.

When the black on black BMW with black tints first pulled up right in front of where she sat, sitting on chrome, Monique wasn't interested, dismissing him as some type of drug dealer. If anything, she was looking for security, and she'd learned long time ago that there was absolutely none in dating a drug dealer, only drugs. Drug money, drug—related people, drug property, which was then all seized when the police or the Feds came and gave out a whole lot of drug time. This was not for her, Monique always told herself, at all.

When Max hopped out, he stood in front of the restaurant with his hands on his hips for a second as though he owned it. Then as soon as he looked over to his right, where she sat, as though she knew him and was waiting for him, he walked right over to her ansd said, "You don't have to wait no more, Shawty, I'm here."

The nerve of this dude, she thought for a second. Never before had anyone ever said anything like that to her before. But as she looked at him, a smile escaped her lips. His confidence was intoxicating. She also noticed that he was tall, about six feet, clean cut, and an irresistable baby face. But she just couldn't get over his cockiness. It was border—line narcissistic, Maybe it was the princess—cut diamonds that flickered in his ears, she figured, or the diamond encrusted pendant that hung on his chain whichwas around his neck. Or, maybe it was his diamond—bezel watch that gave him this type of confidence as he stretched out his hand to introduce himself to her.

"I'm Max," he stated bluntly. "And you, you my Destiny." Monique smiled as her skepticism subsided. She took a chance with his baby face. He didn't talk long, just got her name and told her how fine she was, and how he just couldn't resist the urge to pull over, and when he got out, he couldn't resist coming over and getting to know who this fine specimen of a woman was. And she couldn't resist smiling. He didn't even bother to go in there restaurant, telling her that he was gonna save his appetite for dinner with her at a real restaurant. And that night he took her to Diddy's Justins.

It was then that Monique found out that Max was an independent artist, and that he had just shot two videos, putting them on the internet. When he told her his rap signature, Mad Max, she remembered hearing about him through her best friend, Candace, or other times when her and Candace would go out together. And when she told him about Shawn the cop, he told her, "Shawty, I don't care bout your ex cause I got next. Matter of fact," he continued, "I ain't taking no for an answer. I'm bout to blow like Jigga, and I need my Beyonce in the ride with me."

And so, she got in his ride, moving in with him that very same night. It was drastic but she took a chance. Who was she to judge? Besides, she told herself, she chose him. He didn't choose her.

A year later and they were still holding it down together in spite of. That was the very same house that she was approaching. Wow, that was quick, she thought to herself. Time just seemed to fly as she thought about her man. But then she was little confused. If Max was so busy in the studio laying down tracks, or talking with his manager, Jimmy, then why was his car sitting right there in the driveway?

CHAPTER 4

Monique's stomach felt hollow again. She felt like she wanted to throw up all over the sidewalk. It wouldn't be that bad if he'd answered her call. She looked at her phone. He didn't even text her back.

Maybe Max left something home, she reasoned, as she made her way up the path that led to the front door. Yeah that's it, she thought, putting the keys in the door.

Just inside the house, Monique slammed the door shut. If there was anything going on she didn't want to catch him in the act. She just couldn't stomach anymore surprises for the day. And just as she had expected, Max appeared at the top of the stairs, shirtless and in shorts, revealing his two distinctive burn marks on both shoulders which he had from his childhood. He had no tattoos.

"What's up, babe?" he said with a startled look on his face. "What are you doing here?"

"I got fired," she replied, reading his response real close as she made it up the stairs.

Monique noticed that he looked apprehensive at first, quickly glancing back towards their bedroom, then trying to meet her halfway down the stairs. She also noticed that his skin was sweaty as he came near. He still hadn't responded to her telling him that she was fired.

Just then a woman's voice called from the bedroom. "Max, was that the door?" the voice asked.

Both Max and Monique stood dead in their tracks, reading each other's facial expressions but Monique was the first to respond. "Who was that, Max?" she asked him. She even thought she had recognized the voice.

"It's . . . it's not what you think," Max stuttered. Monique attempted to walk around him but he put his arm up, preventing her. "Wait a minute!"

"Move out my way!" she demanded.

"Calm down first!"

"If it's not what I think, I don't need to calm down."

"Max," the woman's voice summoned. "Are you coming? I know you're not finished already."

Monique then attempted to storm past him. Though the voice was faint because their bedroom was in the back, she was certain she had recognized it that time. Max then grabbed her arm. "Don't make this bigger than it has to be," he told her, now getting serious.

"Get off me!" Monique yanked her arm away.

Just then, in a fit of rage, as if something had gotten into him, Max grabbed her by the throat, slamming her against the wall and choking her. They were still halfway up the stairs.

Monique struggled to move his hands from around her throat but he was far too strong for her. She then tried to yell but couldn't. All the oxygen that was enroute to her brain was being depleted. And her lights were on their way out when the voice called again.

"Max, what's going on?"

"Stay in the room, Candace!" he responded quickly, pushing her.

Simultaneously, as Max shoved Monique, she scratched him but the shove caused her to lose her balance and she tumbled down the stairs, landing in a balled up fetal position at the bottom of the staircase. Her body wasn't moving but her mind was. No, she remembered her mind screaming, not Candace, not her best friend.

CHAPTER 5

The sun had receded permanently for that day, but then the clouds started to form as Pastor Eric Moore exited House of Prayer Church where he pastored for the past ten years. He climbed into his black Toyota Camry, started it up, and was on his way home. Another exciting day serving the Lord, he thought to himself, as he hummed along with Yolanda Adams praising through his speakers.

A few seconds later pastor Moore heard a loud pop, which sounded like a flat tire. "I hope that's not what I think it is," he said, pulling his car over then getting out.

He was tall and slim, brown skin, mid forties or so, young and contemporary looking in dress, for a pastor at least, with sensitive brown eyes.

He walked around the car, looking at the tires. By this time it was just his luck that the rain started falling in dime—sized drops. He sighed, wiping the water from his face as he popped his trunk. When he went around to the back of the vehicle, he heard someone crying off to the right of him. He then turned and headed towards the store in the directions where the sound was coming from but he noticed it was closed.

However, as Pastor Moore peered closer amid the rain drops, towards the right corner of the store, he saw what appeared to be a shadowy figure which looked like a woman secluded in the corner. At first she looked like she was held up under the awning of the store trying to avoid the rain, but as he walked a little closer he noticed that it was her crying. She also had two large black garbage bags by her feet.

"Miss, are you okay?" he asked her.

The woman didn't answer him so Pastor Moore moved slowly towards her. He looked down the block in both directions trying to assess the situation. He thought that maybe she was just robbed, or even worse, raped. But there wasn't anyone in sight, except for an older woman hurrying along with an umbrella. He wiped his face again.

"Miss," Pastor Moore continued, "are you all right?" This time he inched closer, but still maintained a good eight feet distance.

Again there was no response from the woman, just tears.

Pastor Moore took a couple of small steps closer, now able to see the woman's face. She was wearing a black eye, and the other one was swollen. He also noticed that her lip was busted. Her blonde colored hair was frazzled and her orange outfit was soiled with a mixture of blood and dirt. Either she just got into a fight, or this woman made off with someone's drugs and they caught up to her, the pastor thought,

"No, leave me alone!" she finally responded, making eye contact with him.

Pastor Moore just stood there looking at her for a few seconds. He then looked down at her garbage bags, overflowing with clothes and sympathy covered his face. "Can I help you, please?" he pleaded.

The woman backed up even further into the crevice of the store. "No, no, no," she mumbled in between sniffles. Then she started to cry even louder.

"Miss, I think you may need medical attention," he said, inching closer.

She said nothing, just stared back at him.

The pastor looked around and wiped his face again. Then he looked back at her. "I'm Pastor Eric Moore of House of Prayer Church, five blocks from here. Do you know of my church?" She shook her head indicating no. "Okay, can I help you get home or to a family member's house?"

"I don't have a home or any family."

Sighing, Pastor Moore wiped more water from his face. "We need to get out of this rain," he stated. "Would you come back to the church with me?" He waved her to his car as he ran around and climbed into the driver's side. He sat there looking out of the window at this precious soul, clearly in shock. He then mumbled a prayer, "Lord, what shall I do?"

As he looked at her through his car window, he noticed that she was a little more visible than when he first pulled up. She was looking back at him as he sat in the car, but she didn't move from under the store's protective covering. Then she noticed him dial a number on his cell—phone and placed it to the side of his face, still fixing his gaze on her.

❋ ❋ ❋

About ten minutes later, Pastor Eric Moore was now standing in the street talking on his cell-phone as a service truck worker hooked up his car to the truck. The rain was still falling even harder but Pastor Moore was now covered by an umbrella. As he held it over his head he continued to stare at the woman, who was still under the shed of the store.

A couple minutes later another Toyota, this time a white Avalon puleed up behind Pastor Moore's Camry, and the pastor hung up his phone, walking over to the driver's side of the car. In it was his compassionate wife, Barbara. She got out and spoke to him under the umbrella.

"Where is she, hon?" Barbara asked her husband.

Barbara Moore was forty years old. She was an ebony, in its richest sense; a beautiful lustrous black woman, with silky flowing black hair down the center of her back. She exuded class, but the look in her eyes showed that she was indeed a very compassionate woman.

Pastor Moore pointed over to the store. "In front of that store."

Barbara pulled out her umbrella from out of her car and strode confidently over towards the store front as Pastor Moore went over to the service truck. He noticed that the woman still stood motionless but she wasn't crying anymore.

As Barbara approached, she immediately noticed that this young girl was indeed in shock, as her husband had told her over the phone. But Barbara was also shocked to see how battered and bruised she was. Her black eye was almost forced shut. "Hello," Barbara introduced herself. "I'm Barbara Moore. MY husband called me and asked me to come down here." She gestured towards Pastor Moore.

While speaking, Barbara began to choke up looking at this displaced figure. She felt sympathetic. She just couldn't believe that someone would put their hands on such a beautiful girl. Her heart was crying out to the Lord. "I . . . I" she stuttered, then clearing her throat. "I've helped women out of difficult situations before. But it's difficult for me each time," Barbara then began to cry. "Can I help you please, sweetie?"

* * *

Over by the service truck, Tito Lopez, a husky, gruff-looking, service truck operator spoke to Pastor Moore as he attached his car to the truck. "I could've just changed the tire for you, pastor."

"I know, Tito, but it's raining and I want you to check out my brakes also."

"Okay, will do."

"I'll come by the shop tomorrow and pick it up."

As Pastor Moore spoke to Tito, who was nodding his head, he followed Tito's eyes as they both watched Barbara escort the woman to her car. Each woman was carrying a large black garbage bag.

"What's the story with her?" Tito asked the pastor.

"That's what I have to find out."

"Pastor, you're the best," Tito responded with a hug. "I'll see you tomorrow," he added.

"Okay," said Pastor Moore, giving Tito back his umbrella.

Tito then got in the service truck and pulled off as the pastor went and jumped into the passenger side of his wife's car. The woman was in the back seat directly behind the pastor. And Barbara was behind the wheel.

"You wanna take her to the church?" Barbara asked her husband.

"Yes, please," he answered.

As she pulled off, Barbara spoke out loud to Pastor Moore. "Hon, Monique says she doesn't want the police involved. And she doesn't need medical attention."

Pastor Moore turned and got a real good look at the woman for the first time. "Hello, Monique, are you sure?" he asked her. "Because sometimes folks really don't know how severely they've been hurt."

"I'm sure," she responded. "This is not my first time getting hurt."

Monique then stared out the window after saying this. Pastor Moore turned back around glancing at his wife as if to say, We got work to do.

❋ ❋ ❋

Monique sat on the small cot as Barbara stooped down and delicately wiped her face with a wet cloth, as Pastor Moore stood off to the side watching them. They were all in the basement of House of Prayer Church.

The basement was moderately furnished, also very clean and spacious. There was the cot that Monique was sitting on, a small radio on a table next to the cot, and a little bathroom on the side that was equipped with a sink, toilet, and a shower. And in the next room off to the other side there was also a kitchenette.

The two garbage bags with Monique's clothes sat on the side, not too far from the cot.

"There you go," said Barbara, as she stood up and backed up and Pastor Moore stepped forward.

"It's not much," he stated. "But you can rest here." He pointed over to a door. "And the bathroom facility is clean and efficient. Here's my card," he added, digging into his pocket and handing her a card, which she took. It has our home number on it. If you need anything, just call."

Monique still wore a blank stare on her face so pastor Moore wasn't sure if what he said had registered. "If you don't need anything else right now . . ." he continued, searching his wife's face, . . . we'll see you in the morning."

Barbara simply touched her husband's shoulder, gently nudging him to come along. "Get some rest, dear," she told Monique with a smile. Then her and Pastor Moore left. Monique took a second to take in her new environment, then she laid down as a lone tear fell from her eye.